About this book

Sometimes, when Michael Lawrence is asked how old Jiggy McCue is, he says, 'Oh, forty-five, forty-six.' This, of course, is a lie. To prove it, in *Ryan's Brain*, the eighth adventure of the 21st century's very own Three Musketeers, Jiggy celebrates his thirteenth birthday. Celebrates it in a way that *no one* wants to celebrate a birthday, and all because of something he did to his great enemy Bryan Ryan one chilly Wednesday afternoon.

Or rather, something he didn't do . . .

Each Jiggy book is a story in its own right, but if you would like to read them in the order in which they were written, it is:

The Poltergoose, The Killer Underpants,
The Toilet of Doom, Maggot Pie,
The Snottle, Nudie Dudie,
Neville the Devil, Ryan's Brain.

ONE FOR ALL AND ALL FOR LUNCH!

Visit Michael at his website: www.wordybug.com

Ryan's Brain

ORCHARD BOOKS
338 Euston Road, London NW1 3BH
Orchard Books Australia
Hachette Children's Books
Level 17/207 Kent Street, Sydney, NSW 2000
1 84616 227 0
13 digit ISBN: 978 1 84616 227 5
A Paperback Original
First published in 2006 by Orchard Books
Text © Michael Lawrence 2006
Illustrations © Ellis Nadler 2006
The rights of Michael Lawrence to be identified as the author
and of Ellis Nadler to be identified as the illustrator
of this work have been asserted by them in accordance with
the Copyrights, Designs and Patents Act, 1988.
A CIP catalogue record for this book is available from the British Library
5 7 9 10 8 6 4
Printed in Great Britain

Orchard Books is a division of Hachette Children's Books

A JiGGY McCue STORY

Ryan's Brain

Michael Lawrence

ORCHARD BOOKS

This Brain is dedicated to
Cameron Lewis Gee
(even though he doesn't need a spare)

Chapter one

Y'know, some people think it's a real laugh being Jiggy McCue. They do, honestly. Laugh? Ha! They know nothing. My life's a tragedy, day in, day out. Take what happened the week before my thirteenth birthday. Bad enough that my biggest birthday so far was set for a Tuesday during term-time (my parents' warped idea of family planning) but that was nothing compared to what happened in the days leading up to it.

It all started the Wednesday before, at football practice. There I was, that cold, miserable afternoon, shivering in my shorts, fingers crossed over my chest that the ball wouldn't stray my way, no *idea* my life was going to take one of its regular nosedives into the mud in just a few minutes. What kicked the whole thing off was—

No. Wait. Back a bit.

Afternoons have mornings, and I ought to mention the morning of that afternoon because it was the morning of my great experiment. It's a well-known fact that really brilliant people are always misunderstood in their home towns. It probably isn't such a well-known fact that when really brilliant people are kids they're even misunderstood in their own homes. That Wednesday morning is a good example. The scene is my bedroom, my house, the Brook Farm Estate, the crack of seven forty-five. Any time now, my mum will be yelling for me to get up because I'm going to be late AGAIN, then telling me not to gulp my breakfast, to brush my teeth THOROUGHLY, wash my rotten neck, get off to school, and not answer back. You'd think I was some sort of contortionist.

I'd been having a spot of bother getting up recently. Nothing new there, but lately it'd been even harder because the mornings were so dark, and who wants to trade a nice warm bed for a cold dark morning, and school?* It was because of my problem hauling the McCue bod out of the McCue pit on school mornings that I hit on this wheeze to avoid the regular rise-and-shine ear-bashing from the tyrant I'm forced to call Mother, and the

---

* Personally, I don't see why schools can't organise things so lessons begin after lunch, but don't get me started.

ticking-off from Face-Ache Dakin when I'm late for registration. Half my trouble is finding the extra minutes to kick my PJs into a corner and slot myself into my stupid uniform, so what I thought was, what if I delete the switch from night-clothes to day-clothes? I don't mean go to school in my pyjamas, I mean be already dressed when I wake up. Save quite a wad of time, you have to agree.

Well, that's the plan I put into action the night before that Wednesday. My school jacket and shoes were already downstairs, and my school tie (still knotted) was round the neck of Roger my gorilla, so that in the morning I could just slip it off him and on me. But I was still in everything else when I got into bed that Tuesday night, and wishing I'd thought of it years ago. What I didn't count on was being so snug and warm when my *Nightmare Before Christmas* alarm went off in the morning that I would cover my head and shunt right back to dreamland. Or that my mother would run in to wake me without waiting for a 'Yes, please, fine, do come in, you're so welcome.'

'Jiggy!' she screeched. 'You'll be late again!'

Then she tugged the duvet back. And saw...

13

'Jiggy, you didn't go to bed in your *school* clothes!'

I screwed my bright morning eyes into place.

'Are you kidding?' Course not. I was up ages ago, got dressed, then thought I'd just lie down for a sec...'

She wasn't buying it. Sometimes you can fool my mother easy as gooseberry pie, other times you might as well leave the room and let her get on with it. Except I couldn't leave the room yet because she might have noticed she was just nagging herself.

'I can't believe you went to bed fully dressed,' she said.

'Fully dressed?' I said. 'No, look. No jacket, no shoes, and Roger's wearing my tie.'

'Don't play games with me, young man,' she chuntered. 'You're in bed in your school clothes. Have you any idea where those things have *been*?'

'Well, they've been to school a few times. Apart from that, ask me another.'

'I just don't believe you've done this,' she said.

'Yeah, I got that,' I said. 'Can I go down for my Super Choco Bombs now?'

'There'll be dust on them.'

'Why? Dad left the packet open again? I've told him not to do that. I've also told him not to *eat* my cereal, but there's no reasoning with that man.'

'I'll have to change the sheets and duvet cover,' Mum said. 'They'll be filthy.'

'They're filthy anyway, you're always telling me.'

'I don't understand you, Jiggy, I really don't.'

'I can speak more slowly if you like.'

'You actually wore your school clothes to *bed*.'

'This is where we came in,' I said. 'Where you came in. Which was for...?'

'To get you up so you wouldn't be late for school.'

'Hey, that's the reason I was wearing my togs in bed!' I cried. 'Great minds, eh?'

She shook her head slowly from side to side. 'School clothes in bed,' she said, 'school clothes in bed,' like her voice was on a loop.

'I'll say it again,' I said patiently. 'I only wore these few things. Not the full shebang. To save *time*.'

'Whether you wore all your clothes or just some of them in bed is quite beside the point,' Mum said.

'What point's that then?'

15

'You know very well what point. The point under discussion.'

'People are always saying that,' I said.

'Saying what?'

'That things are beside the point. Everything can't be beside the point. If everything was beside the point there might as well not *be* a point. The point would be out of a job. It would feel pointless. Have to go out and look for new work, as a window cleaner maybe, or a nagging mother.'

'Jiggy, you do talk nonsense.'

'It's a gift,' I said. 'Now are we done here or is this going on till bedtime?'

She let me go, but all through breakfast she went on about me wearing my school clothes in bed. Even when I went to the bathroom she had her mouth against the door, saying 'Jiggy this, Jiggy that, I just don't believe you, school clothes, bed, filthy, blah, blah,' and when I went downstairs again she wouldn't let me out of the house till she'd gone through the whole scene a wackillion times more. And guess what.

I was late for school.

16

Chapter Two

I usually go to school with Pete and Angie because they're my best friends and they live just across the road, but because I was late they'd gone on ahead, so I went on my own that day. I wasn't the only late kid. One of the others was Eejit Atkins from next door, but when I spotted him I hung back so I wouldn't have to walk with him, which made me later still. There were a couple of others I knew on the way, but only one other from my class. This was Bryan Ryan, who I bumped into in the shopping centre. I bumped into him because he was standing just round the corner drooling over something in the sports shop window.

'Watch where you're going, McCue!' he snapped.

'Watch where you're standing, Ryan!' I snapped back.

We don't get on, Ryan and I, never have, but sometimes I have a bit of fun with him and he doesn't realise. I had some a few weeks before the

Wednesday I'm telling you about. It was a Saturday and I was in town with my dad. I don't make a habit of going shopping with either of my parents if I can charm my way out of it, but Dad and I had vouchers left over from Christmas and Mum said we ought to use them before the companies went into receivership, whatever that is. Unfortunately, my vouchers were for books (they came from my gran, who's crazy) so I might as well have torn them up, and Dad's were for clothes, and Dad goes into snooze mode whenever he has to choose clothes, so we'd ended up in the audio-visual section of this big department store called Turpin's. Dad says Turpin's overprice everything, calls them highway robbers, but he was happy enough to stand with this row of other sad men watching some blonde female in a leotard doing stretching exercises on a stack of huge TVs. I was waiting for him to lose interest when I spotted Ryan. He was in camouflaged army-type trousers and matching jacket, staring at a portable TV with a built-in DVD player. The TV was camouflaged the same way, green and brown, like bushes and ground from the air. There was a war film on the screen. Ryan's into war.

'I thought I saw Ryan here just now,' I said, sneaking up, standing near him, looking the other way. 'Must have imagined it.'

Ryan turned. 'Get lost, McCue.'

'Now I hear his *voice*!' I cried in amazement. 'Where can it be *coming* from?

'How do you fancy wearing a neck brace?' Ryan asked.

I whirled round. Stared at him in pretend surprise.

'There you are! Hey, that camouflage outfit really works. Not thinking of buying a TV to match, are you? For your bedroom maybe? Hope you don't have camouflage wallpaper too. If you have camouflage wallpaper you'll never be able to find a TV like that to turn it on.'

'McCue,' Ryan said, 'you're a plonker.'

'Maybe I am,' I replied, fast as a ferret, 'but at least I'm not a camouflaged one.'

That's the kind of conversation I have with Bry-Ry all the time. Nearest I get to enjoying his company.

Back to that Wednesday.

When I'm averagely late for school I join the last fifty or so cramming through the gates as the bell goes, but this late it wasn't such a battle. A teacher was waiting for late-comers. A teacher who looked like he wished he was allowed to carry a whip.

'Move it, Ryan, Shah, McCue, and you, whatever your name is!'

This teacher was one of the school shouters. There are a few of those at Ranting Lane. The kind who shout at you for breathing. Our best teachers don't shout much. Sometimes, yes, all right, maybe they have reason to *sometimes*, but not whenever they move their lips. Take Mrs Gamble, who has us for English. Mrs Gamble loses it occasionally, like when we suddenly start chucking things at one another when it isn't part of the lesson, but she doesn't shout for the sake of it. And Mr Lubelski, our Art teacher, he never shouts. I think Mr Lubelski's more nervous of us than we are of him. Mr Dent's another teacher who doesn't bully us. Mr D tries to teach us how to make things out of wood and stuff. Most of us are about as clever at things like that as snails are at formation flying, but he doesn't seem to mind. Teachers like those three and a few others are good. Teachers who shout at kids for nothing aren't so good. They should be doing something other than teaching. They should be Town Criers or something, who get *paid* for shouting.

Here are some of the things the Shouting Teachers of Ranting Lane come out with most often. Stop me if any of them sound familiar.

'SIT STILL!'

'SILENCE!'

'ANSWER WHEN I SPEAK TO YOU!'

'DON'T ANSWER BACK!'

'SPEAK UP, BOY!'

'YOU PEOPLE DON'T KNOW YOU'RE BORN!'*

'I SAW THAT!'

'I HEARD THAT!'

'WHO MADE THAT SMELL?'

'SINGLE FILE!'

'STOP THAT PUSHING!'

'GET OUT OF MY SIGHT!'

'DON'T RUN, WALK!'

'DON'T DAWDLE!'

'THINK, BOY, THINK!'

'SEE ME AFTER CLASS!'

---

* What does that *mean*?

'I'VE NEVER SEEN SUCH A FEEBLE PERFORMANCE IN MY LIFE!'

The last of these is yelled all the time by Mr Rice, who takes us for games. Mr Rice hardly ever speaks quietly to us boys, and he wears these enormous trainers and a red tracksuit at all times. I don't know if it's always the same tracksuit or if he has a whole rack of identical ones, but the only time I've seen him in anything else is out of school, when I try to avoid him even more than I do *at* school. Mr Rice and I are not soul-mates. He thinks that if a boy isn't mad about football there's something wrong with him. My dad thinks that too. My father is very disappointed that the footie gene missed me.

Mr Rice was there the afternoon this thing happened. Second session of the week with him, which is two too many. Like I said at the start, it was football practice, which took place on the playing field, surprise-surprise. I don't like the playing field. Being on it, I mean. Feels like an arena because there are houses along most of one side, and people sometimes stand in their back gardens or bedroom windows watching us make newts of ourselves.

Anyway, there I am in my regulation black shorts and red shirt, plus a green sash (half of us were in a green sash, the other half in a blue one), as close to the sidelines as I can get without going home, no idea that I'm experiencing the best bit of the next seven days of my life. If I'd known this I might have enjoyed it more. Might have run up and down shouting 'THIS IS THE HIGHLIGHT, I AM SO **LOVING** IT!' But I didn't know it, so I stayed put, hugging myself with misery while my knees tapped out a rhythm I didn't recognise. On another part of the field the girls were playing hockey. I envied them. Not because they were playing hockey, but because Miss Weeks took them for it, and Miss Weeks doesn't scream at them all the time. Also, because if they got bored they could trip someone up with their sticks for a laugh. There were no laughs on the footie pitch. None at all. I tried to merge with the non-existent scenery, keeping well out of it while Mr Rice charged about blowing his stupid whistle and shouting at everyone to do better. It wasn't until Ryan got the ball that his loud sneers changed to loud cheers.

Ryan lives for football and is always trying to show how great he is at it, which goes down pretty well with the Sugar Ricicle.

As the action had moved right away from me, I felt free to wander to the nearest goal. I needed something to lean against and goals have posts, which are made for leaning in spite of the rumours. With all the heavy foot stuff occurring down the other end I reckoned I stood a fair chance of a couple of minutes' peace. There were only two other boys up this end now. One was Martin Skinner, in goal and a blue sash. Skinner's about as good a goalie as I am, but everyone has to take a turn, even me and him.

'Mind if I lean here a while, Sir Skinnerlot?' I asked politely.

'Lean on your own goal,' he replied.

'Thanks.' I jammed my back against the post.

The other boy this end was Golden Boots himself, Ryan, who wore the same colour sash as me today. Ryan and me on the same side. Only in football practice! Now that he'd shown the others how to do it, he was running on the spot while waiting for the ball to come back. When it did, he would pin Skinner to the back of the net with it and run round with his arms in the air while Mr Rice shouted, 'Nice one, Ryan, nice one!'

'Hey, number eight!' I called. 'You wanna watch that spot running. That's how acne starts.'

Yes, I know, pretty lame, but I was bored.

Ryan turned. 'You talking to me, McCue?'

'I am if you answer to number eight.'

'That's my shirt's number.'

'Your *shirt's* number? Are all your shirts numbered, Ryan?'

'If you really want to know, eight's my lucky number.'

'Oh, right. Had me worried there. Thought for a sec you'd got one for every day of the week, and no one'd told you the week stops at seven.'

'Ho-ho-ho,' he said. 'What about you then – number 13?'

I couldn't deny that I was the only other kid with a number on his shirt, and that the number was thirteen. Ryan gets away with it because he's the Ricicle's favourite, I get away with it because my mum can't get it out. It was Garrett's doing. He'd put it there with an indelible marker pen

25

one day when my back was turned. Soon that number would be quite appropriate, but once I'd celebrated my 13th birthday I intended to get some hairy legs from Help the Aged and shoot up to six nine, so I could burn the shirt and jump on the ashes.

Couldn't let Ryan get one up on me, though.

'Y'know, it's amazing,' I said to him.

'What is?' he said, gulping the bait like a starving trout.

'Here we are, century twenty-one, footprints on the moon, a thousand TV channels at the touch of a button, crisps every flavour in the universe, and people still kick balls into enormous hairnets. Crazy or *what*?'

Ryan scowled. Trash his favourite sport and he's likely to slam you against a wall and introduce a knee to your Titch and Quackers. But I didn't care. I was fed up, I was cold, I was watching my life dribble by on a footie field when I could have been at home, near a radiator, chortling at a comic.

'How would you like a good thump, McCue?' Ryan asked.

This wasn't a very bright question. Even he

should have known there was only one answer to a question like that.

'That'd be great,' I said, folding my arms over my number thirteen. 'Long as it's a *good* thump. It's the bad ones I hate.'

He snarled. Started towards me. 'I'm serious.'

I wriggled my spine on the goalpost. 'Really? Well, you had me fooled. You're a natural comedian, you know that? A real stand-up. Ever thought of going into that line of...? Oh. Forgot. You tried it, but everyone laughed.'

Now you might think I was pushing my luck a bit here, but there were at least six seconds between me saying this and Ryan doing his worst. I can almost always get out of a hammering from Ryan by saying something cute in the closing seconds.

I was about to start on this when Skinner said, 'What's going on there?' He was pointing down the pitch. At the far end, near the other goal, almost every boy was piling on top of almost every other boy and Mr Rice was wading in to haul them apart.

'The beautiful game,' I said with a sigh.

The only one of the three of us who wasn't

fascinated by the scene was Ryan. He only had eyes for me. Mean eyes. And he was getting closer.

Time to distract him.

'Did I ever tell you about my Uncle Bob, the professional footballer?'

He stopped like an invisible wall had popped up in front of him.

'Professional footballer?'

'Yes. I ever mention him?'

He squinted suspiciously.

'*You've* got an uncle who's a pro footballer?'

'Yeah. Well, he was. With one of the big national teams.'

'What team?'

'What team?'

Suddenly I couldn't remember the name of any of them.

'Yeah, who'd he play for?'

Time to wing it. 'The one with the blue and white shirts?'

Ryan's jaw almost cracked his chest.

'Wow.'

Bob's your uncle. Or my uncle. Except I didn't actually have an Uncle Bob. But Bry-Ry didn't need to know that. Didn't want to know it either. He wanted to hear about a relative who'd hit the big-time, become rich and famous, maybe got a knighthood for kicking balls. I could have given him something along those lines, but it would have been too easy, no fun at all. So...

'Yes,' I said. 'Uncle Bob. Real soccer hero. On TV the whole time. People travelled from all over to see him play. Signed shed-loads of autographs.'

'But he's not still playing?' Ryan said, wishing he had an uncle like that, even a retired one.

'No. Gave it up a while back.'

'What, too old?'

'No, no. He was at his peak when he hung up his boots.'

Ryan's amazement was a wonder to behold. 'He was a star player and he gave it *up*? Why?'

'So he could take that job,' I said.

'What job?'

'Disinfecting the Shopping Centre public toilets. He says it's so much more worthwhile than running round a field looking for someone to hug.'

Ryan's eyes turned to rat droppings. He stepped closer, but not waving his knuckles like I thought he would. My little jest had messed with his head, and that head wanted to get its own back.

Now Ryan's head is no ordinary head. Ordinary heads don't spend every spare hour of daylight butting footballs. Ryan's head must have butted a thousand footballs in its time. But a head that butts a thousand footballs isn't only good for butting footballs. It also comes in handy for butting the heads of people who try to pull one of its owner's legs. I could tell that's what Ryan planned to do now. Lob his head at mine to teach it a lesson.

And here's where my latest disaster started.

Just before Ryan's head turned mine to mashed swede, I decided that staying where I was probably wasn't such a great idea and stepped smartly to my left. His feet were already off the ground when I did this, so it was too late for him to stroke his chin thoughtfully and murmur, 'Hmm, maybe I'd better reconsider my action here.'

When I heard his skull crack against the goalpost I'd been leaning against, one of my nervous jigs kicked in.*

When he gave a funny little sigh, dropped to his knees and keeled over with his peach in the

* In times of stress my feet dance. Sometimes my elbows flap too. That's why I'm called Jiggy. You probably knew that. If not, why not? Everyone else does.

30

air, the jig picked up even more.

By the time the peach sagged and he was stretched out on the ground I was jigging like a maniac.

'YOU BOYS! WHAT'S GOING ON UP THERE?!'

I managed to get my feet under control. Stood looking down at my arch-enemy, face down in the grass, spark out to the world.

At the figure eight on his back.

And that was his *lucky* number?

Chapter Three

It had gone all quiet down the other end. Mr Rice was running towards us like a giant bullet in a tracksuit.

'What happened?!' he shouted as he zoomed up.

'Well,' I said, 'Ryan sort of—'

'Out of the way, boy!'

He threw himself down on one knee and hooked one of Ryan's wrists, groped it, found what he was looking for, and dropped it back on the grass. 'Whew!' he said, getting to his feet. 'Thought he'd copped it there for a sec!'

Maybe it was the dropping of his wrist that made the next thing happen, I don't know, but as it hit the ground Ryan's whole body twitched and the hand attached to the wrist jerked sideways and grabbed my ankle. I tried to pull away, but I couldn't. Ryan had quite a grip, even unconscious.

'Geddimoffme!' I said, struggling.

But then the hand went all floppy and I quickstepped out of reach before it could grab me again. I could still feel that grip, though, and a sort of tingle where it had been.

Mr Rice's eyes were slits as he looked down at me. 'What did you do to him, McCue?!'

'Do?' I said. 'I didn't do anything.'

'Oh! Is that a fact!'

I looked around for someone to back me up. There was only Skinner, sitting on the ground near the other end of the goal.

'I didn't, did I, Skinner?'

Skinner glanced at me, and glanced away again.

'Didn't see. Wasn't watching.'

Not someone you turn to in a crisis, Skinner.

Rice shouted the names of two of the nearer boys as the rest of the herd trotted towards us. 'Go to reception, you two, tell them to get an ambulance down here right away! Go, go, quick, no time to waste!'

Wapshott and Aziz loped up the slope to do as they were told. Rice turned back to me.

'You have some explaining to do, boy!'

'But I didn't *do* anything!' I protested.

'Well, that has to be *proved*!' he said. '*Doesn't* it now?!'

While we were waiting for the ambulance we stood around in small shivery groups not saying much. Even the Ricecake, standing with Miss Weeks, had put the shouts on hold. But all eyes kept drifting back to me, and that bothered me.

When the ambulance arrived they had to drive it very carefully between the school buildings because they're so close together, and down the slope to the field and us at the far end of it. The ambulance men turned Ryan over, lifted him onto a stretcher, covered him to the chin with a blanket, and slid him inside. As the ambulance trundled back up the hill, leaving deep tracks in Mr Rice's precious grass, Pete sidled up to me.

'Finally did it then, eh, Jig?'

'Did what?'

'Put Ryan's lights out.'

'He put 'em out himself, nothing to do with me.'

'How'd he manage that?'

'Banged his head on the goalpost. Meant to do a header on me, but I moved aside.'

'You moved aside so he wouldn't butt you?'

'Yeah. Wouldn't you have?'

'And he cracked his head on the goalpost?'

'Got it, Pete. Take a gold star.'

'So you did put his lights out.'

My forehead dropped over my eyes, the way Rice's does when he talks to me sometimes.

'I did not put the pumpkin's lights out. If he hadn't tossed his head at me, I wouldn't have moved, and he wouldn't have smacked it on the post and be in the back of that ambulance on the way to hospital under a blanket.'

'Exactly,' Pete said.

'What do you mean, exactly?'

'If you hadn't moved, he'd still be here.'

'Yes,' I said. 'And it'd be me in the ambulance.'

'Not necessarily.'

'Yes necessarily. Ryan's head is not made of rubber. It might look like it, but it's not. Nor's the goalpost. And my head would have been between those two very hard objects. Look, I'll show you.'

I put one hand behind his head, but not touching. Put my other hand in front of his face, about six noses away.

Pete flinched. 'What are you doing?'

35

'Stand still. The hand behind your head's the goalpost, right?'

'Riiiight,' he said nervously.

'And the hand in front of your face is Ryan's head, right?'

'Um…'

'Now Ryan's head's coming at you like it wants to turn your face to peanut butter, yes?'

'Peanut butter?'

I smacked him sharply on the forehead with the palm in front of it. He yelped as his bonce flew into the hand behind it.

'Head sandwich,' I said. 'Except the head wouldn't be between bread – or hands – it'd be between a head that's butted a thousand footballs and a length of wood that someone painted white about twenty years ago.'

'McCue!!!'

I knew that name. I also knew that voice. I looked around. Mr Rice was lumbering towards me again.

'Sir?'

'What is it with you today, McCue?! Declared war on the whole class, have you?!'

'No, sir, I was just showing Garrett how–'

'Showing him what?!' He skidded to a halt just short of me and about three metres above me. 'How you put Ryan into a coma?!'

'C-coma?' I stammered.

'The boy's unconscious!' he screamed.

'Yeah, but…coma? Doesn't that mean…?'

'It means he might *stay* unconscious! Let's see you worm your way out of this one! In the meantime, do not – I say DO NOT – attack anyone else – d'you hear me?!?!?!'

Hear him? A deaf person three fields away would have heard him. Mr Rice marched back to where Miss Weeks was standing with Angie and some of the other girls. Miss Weeks sometimes wears a shorty skirt and knickers like the girls, but today she was in a bright green tracksuit with a yellow stripe down the leg. She didn't look so great in it because of the bump in her front. When we first started to notice the bump a while back we thought she was putting on weight. Angie said a few of the girls, including her, got in some digs about exercise being a good idea, or maybe less pasta, and Miss Weeks just smiled, and gradually it sank in that the extra weight she was carrying wasn't her own.

After a bit of a conflab between the Weeks and the Ricicle, they told us to go back to the changing rooms, even though the lesson still had twenty minutes to go. Up in the changing room I discovered that Pete wasn't the only one who thought I'd knocked Ryan out, which meant a mixture of praise and blame. The praise would have been OK if I'd really done it, but Ryan's sporty friends weren't so happy with me, and nobody – praisers or blamers – believed me when I said I wasn't responsible.

I was just about to strip off and run madly into the showers like all the others when Mr Rice looked out of his little office and shouted that we had to go see Mr Hubbard.

'What, all of us?' I said.

'Just you and me, McCue!'

'Why?'

'To explain what you did to Ryan!'

'I didn't do anything to Ryan, I told you.'

'Well, now you can tell the Head! Get changed!'

'What about my shower?'

'Have one at home! Change, McCue!'

I got changed and we marched to Mother Hubbard's office. Mr R didn't say a word the whole way, but out of the corner of my eye I saw him giving me these nasty looks every few steps.

The Head's secretary, Miss Prince, was expecting us. She sent us straight in. Mr Rice closed the door behind us very quietly, which made me gulp a bit. It felt so serious, the door closing that quietly. I didn't get any less gulpy when every eye in the room looked at me – Mr Hubbard's, Mr Rice's, the spotted dog's in the calendar on the wall. Mother, sitting behind his desk, rolling a pencil across it, asked me for 'a full account of what happened out there'. I told him as much as he needed to know. That I'd just been standing by the goal and Ryan had jumped at me and I'd got out of the way and he'd smacked his dome.

'You didn't hit him then,' he said.

I made a shocked face. 'Hit him? No, sir!'

'You simply...moved?'

'Yes. That's all.'

'Pull the other one, McCue!'

This was Mr Rice, and even though it wasn't quite his usual shout because we were in the

Head's office he somehow made it sound like one. This narked me. That man always thinks I'm up to something even when I'm not.

'I didn't do *anything*!' I said.

'Oh! Really!'

'Yes! Really!'

'I think,' Mr Hubbard said to Mr Rice, 'that we must give the lad the benefit of the doubt here. There's no evidence of any misdemeanour, after all.'

'Evidence!' Rice said, firing hot daggers at me. 'McCue and Ryan are always at each other's throats. Doesn't it strike you as a bit of a coincidence that the moment my back's turned one of them ends up *unconscious*?'

Mr Hubbard looked at Mr Rice. He didn't seem too pleased about something. 'Joseph,' he said, still looking at Mr R, 'wait outside for a minute please.'

'Jiggy,' I said.

'What?' he said.

'My name,' I said. 'Jiggy. As in McCue.'

'Just wait outside, will you?'

I slid out the door, glad to oblige.

'Done already?' Miss Prince asked me.

'Mother told me to wait here.'

'Your mother?'

'Mr Hubbard.'

'Oh. Well, you'd better take a seat.'

'Where?' I said.

'What?' she said.

'Where do you want me to take it?'*

'Just *sit*,' she said, like someone with their neck in a vice.

I sat down on a chair against the wall and she went back to whatever she was doing on her desk. I asked if there was anything to read. She said it wasn't a dentist's waiting room. I said, 'Glad to hear it,' and shoved my hands in my pockets, gazed around at nothing.

In a minute, Mr Rice opened the door.

'McCue! In!'

I got up. Went back into the office. Rice closed the door behind me, not so quietly this time, and went to stand beside Hubbard's desk again. He hadn't looked in such a terrific mood before, but he looked in an even less terrific one now, like he'd been told off for something and didn't like it. Mr Hubbard leant forward and looked at me very seriously.

---

* I can't seem to help it. I think it's an illness.

'We have decided,' he said, and when Mr Rice cleared his throat he started again, with a sort of edge to his voice. '*I* have decided to take your word for what happened today and say no more about it.'

'You have?' I said. This was a first. Teachers taking my word? I ought to have asked for a certificate for my bedroom wall.

'Yes. Though I hope that in future you'll be more careful during Games.'

'I promise never to move on the playing field again,' I said.

Mr Rice growled deep in his sarcophagus.

'Good lad,' said Mr Hubbard, to me I think, not Mr Rice. 'Run along now.'

I didn't run, I backed out, only just managing not to bow. Because Mother H had said I could go, I went – home, even though the bell hadn't gone. I knew that if I hung around waiting for official home-time there'd be questions from everyone I met. I'd had all the questions I could deal with for one Wednesday.

Chapter Four

First thing I did when I got home was go upstairs and run a bath. Running baths isn't something I do that often if I can help it. I think too much water on your body is bad for you. Look at really ancient Golden Oldies. Lifetime of baths, full-body wrinkles, disgusting. So why take a bath when I haven't been ordered into it? Because I needed to lie somewhere warm, with a bolted door between me and the world. It was Ryan, of course. What happened might not have been my fault, but like Pete said, if I hadn't moved he would only have cracked his head on mine and probably not be in hospital now. Either that or we both would. I wouldn't have admitted it to anyone, but that bothered me a smidgen.

I don't know how long I was in the bath. I was playing with my little diving duck in the bubbles – most fun I'd had all day – and it was taking my mind off what had happened quite well until I heard the front door slam. Half a minute later, Mum was yelling up the stairs.

'Jiggy? You in?'

'No!'

Footsteps coming up.

'Where are you?'

'Bathroom!'

'What are you doing in there?'

'How many guesses do you want?'

'Why are your clothes all over the landing?'

'I'm taking a bath.'

I heard a gasp. 'You're taking a bath? *You're* taking a *bath*? Without being *told* to?'

'Showers weren't working after Games,' I lied. 'Thought you'd want me to wash the mud off. Why are you home so early?'

'I had to see someone near here. The day was getting on, so I came home. I'll put some clean clothes out for you.'

Clean clothes. My mother's a fanatic about clean clothes. She'd have me changing every half hour if I let her.

'No!' I said. 'It's all right!' I said. 'Don't bother!' I said.

Silence. She was gone. I might as well have

44

been talking to my duck.

I threw myself over the side of the bath and pulled the plug. Dried myself on the lifesize Johnny Depp bath towel I've been forbidden to use, grabbed my dressing gown from the hook on the door, and went to my room, where...

Clean togs laid out on my bed, as neat as a shop display − in the order I had to put them on. The ones nearest the door were the new underpants my gran gave me for Christmas along with the useless book tokens. I'm not a huge fan of new underpants, but these were covered in comicbook superheroes showing their muscles, or flying, or swinging on bits of rope. Quite neat really.

I inserted a foot into leghole one, tugged upward, dipped my second foot into hole two, hauled all the way. They fitted a treat. More than a treat. They were really snug. I mean *really* snug. Then I got it. The thinking behind them. A lot of superheroes wear snug pants like these. Maybe not with pictures of other heroes all over them, but just as body-hugging.

I tried strolling round the room. It wasn't easy. The material was so huggy you had to walk like a knight in armour who's lost his horse. I tried sitting. Ho! I got up. The material stayed where it had no right to be. This must be what it felt like wearing a thong. I screwed my head over my shoulder to peer at my kazoo in the long mirror on the wall. The pants were so much a part of me that if not for the bright colours and the heroes you wouldn't have known I had anything on at all.

I was still marvelling at this when Mum threw the door back like she was the last one up the gangplank for a round-the-world cruise. 'How are the new pants?' she demanded.

I grabbed my Fat Pig money box and covered my front loot.

'What have I told you about knocking?' I said fiercely.

'I don't know,' she said. 'What have you told me about knocking?'

'I mean, *do* it! Knock, wait, go away when I don't answer. Dad's got the hang of it, why haven't you?'

'I'm your mother.'

'That's no excuse. Go!'

'I just wanted to know what your gran's pants are like.'

'How would I know? Ask her.'

'I mean the ones she...' She trailed off. She'd seen my superheroic back end in the mirror. 'Er... how do they feel?'

I stepped sideways to ruin her view.

'Like a transfer,' I said. 'What are these things *made* of?'

'Lycra,' she said, and spun out of the room like a top.

I would have taken the pants off right then and put some comfy old ones on, but when I looked in my underwear drawer there weren't any. My mother must have expected this and cleared it out so I'd have to give the new ones a chance. I cursed and put on the other things she'd laid out for me.

By the time I was dressed I was hungry. Long time since lunch. I went downstairs. Slowly. Weird experience, going down in those pants. All I could think of all the way, all I could feel, was the material cuddling my secret bits. I wondered if lycra is what male ballet dancers' tights are made of, and if they are, how do they move in them? Practice, I suppose. Even with practice the lycra would keep everything except the dancers' legs from moving, but that's probably just as well or the audience would be put off their popcorn. I might also have wondered why they would wear lycra tights in the first place (instead of loose-fitting dungarees, say) but I'd made it to the kitchen by then and lost interest.

I was trying to stoop in my superhero underpants to raid the Assorted Broken Biscuits tin when the doorbell went.

'Get that will you, Jiggy?!' my mother yodelled from upstairs.

I did my knight-of-old-without-a-horse walk to the hall and called up the stairs – softly, so whoever was on the doorstep wouldn't hear. 'Can you get it? I don't want to see anyone.'

Silence. She hadn't heard. The bell went again. Mum came to the top of the stairs.

'Jiggy! The door!'

'Why can't you answer it?' I whispered.

'What?' she said, leaning over from on high.

I raised my voice – 'It's probably for you' – just enough for her to make out the words.

This time she got it, just. But she wasn't

interested. 'If it's for me, call me and I'll come down. Until then I'll stay here, making your bed and tidying up after you in the bathroom.'

I sighed. The pressures of life! I opened the door. It wasn't someone for Mum, it was someone for me. Two someones. Pete and Angie. I knew this wasn't a social call. Like half the school, they'd have questions.

'Where were you?' Pete asked, getting right to it.

'Where was I when?'

'At afternoon registration? After school?'

'I was here.'

'Mr Dakin wasn't pleased.'

'Mr Dakin's never pleased.'

'What did you do to Ryan?' This was Angie.

'I didn't do anything to Ryan, ask Pete.'

'Why ask Pete?'

'Because I've been through this with him already.'

She frowned at him. 'You didn't say.'

He shrugged a shoulder. 'Didn't ask.'

'Why would I ask if I didn't know you knew?'

He shrugged the other shoulder. Angie turned back to me. 'It's cold out here.'

'It's winter,' I said, and would have closed the door if she hadn't pushed it back and shoved past me, followed by Pete.

'Now,' she said, shutting the door. 'Tell me about Ryan.'

'Tell you what about Ryan?'

'What you did to put him in hospital.'

'I did not put Ryan in hospital. Repeat. I did not. Put Ryan. In hospital.'

'Why's he there then?'

'Maybe he likes the food.'

'I want the whole story,' Angie said.

'Well I don't want to tell it.'

'Well you're going to,' she said. 'Upstairs.'

'I don't want to go upstairs.'

'Up-*stairs*!'

I started up. No use arguing when she's in that sort of mood.

'Why are you walking like that?' she asked half way. She was just behind me, a couple of steps down.

'Like what?

'All stiff, like you've got a tent pole up your jacksie.'

'Maybe he's got a tent pole up his jacksie,' Pete said from behind her.

'If you must know,' I said, 'it's my gran's underpants.'

'You're wearing your gran's underpants?' Angie said.

'The ones she gave me for Christmas.'

'Oh, you and your underpants. What this time?'

'Hang on.'

I said 'Hang on' because I didn't want my mother tuning in. The bathroom door was open. She was leaning over the bath scrubbing the tidemark I'd considerately made for her so she'd feel useful. We tiptoed into my room, where I closed the door firmly and told them about the superhero pants that fitted me like a rubber glove without fingers and a thumb.

'Let's see,' Pete said.

'Sure,' I replied. 'Soon as hell freezes over.'

'Why can't I see?'

'Why do you think?'

I glanced at Angie. A glance was all it took.

'Oh, I see,' she said, chucking her nose in the air. 'The old boy-girl divide rears its ugly head yet again.'

'Ange,' I said. 'This is personal stuff. As personal as it gets.'

This didn't bring her nose down much. 'It's just underwear. I've seen you in your underwear before.

'Not underwear like this, you haven't. These things are so clingy I'm embarrassed to be in them even with my jeans on. They get into corners I didn't know I had, and as for sitting down in them…now I know why superheroes spend so much time standing up and leaping off tall buildings. Only thing to do in lycra pants.'

'You could be a superhero,' Pete said, flopping across the bed my mother had just made.

'What?' I said.

'Got the pants, what else do you need?'

Angie parked herself in my only chair. 'The odd power might be a good idea. And a body that doesn't look like it was modelled out of papier maché by a six year old.'

'He could call himself Captain Underpants,' Pete said.

'Been done,' I grunted, looking for something to lean on.

'We could all get lycra undies and be superheroes.'

Pete again. 'The three of us. Superheroes instead of Musketeers.* Capes and boots, the works. Get ourselves some really natty outfits.'

'Was that natty or nutty?' I said, longing to pull the two halves of my backside apart and yank those pants back where they belonged.

'Superheroes are older than us,' Angie said. 'Look at Hellboy. Forty if a day. Some boy.'

'There are some young superheroes,' Pete said. 'Look at Peter Parker.'

'The paperboy?'

'Spiderman. Should be Spider*boy*, his age.'

I gave in. Giving in's the only thing to do when conversations this mindless look like they're not going to end any time soon.

'We could call ourselves by our initials,' I said.

'Initials?' said Pete.

'Yes. J-Man for me – Jig-man, see? – and you could be P-Boy, and Angie could be A-Girl.'

'A-Girl?' Angie said. 'That's the same as "a girl". How heroic is A Girl?'

'Depends how you say it. And how you look. If you stick your little chest out and put your hands on your waist and drop your voice to

---

* In case you don't know, we're a secret society called The Three Musketeers. We've been Musketeers since we were so high. Can't remember whose idea it was. Not sure I want to in case it was mine.

hero-level, and say "I am A-Girl" it could sound quite cool.'

'Could also sound quite naff. If I ever become a superhero remind me not to ask some tadpole in lycra called J-Man for name suggestions.'

'And if you think I'm gonna be P-Boy,' Pete grouched, 'you can go home right now.'

'Pete,' I said. 'I am home. This is my room.' He looked around. He'd forgotten that. 'For you,' I said, 'an even better name would be Captain Pea-Brain.'

'Talking of brains,' Angie said. 'Someone at school said Ryan could have brain damage.'

I felt the blood drain from my cheeks. All four of them.

'Brain damage?'

'So she said.'

'Who?'

'Marlene Bronson.'

'Marlene Bronson? What does she know?'

'Her mum's a nurse.'

'Maybe she is, but her mum wasn't there.'

'No, but what if she's right? What if Ryan does have brain damage?'

'How would you tell with Ryan?' said Pete.

'You shouldn't mock someone in that condition,' Angie said.

'Why not?'

'Because you shouldn't.'

'Well, even with brain damage Ryan'd be all right,' Pete said.

'How'd you work that out?'

'He only wants to be a footballer.'

Chapter Five

I couldn't get Ryan out of my head after Pete and Angie went home. Couldn't help imagining how different it might have been if I'd let him butt me instead of the goalpost. If that had happened, it could have been me unconscious on the ground and him the one blamed for hospitalising a classmate. Bet Mr Rice wouldn't have blamed him, though. I could imagine the way it would have gone.

'Ryan, what happened to McCue?!'

'Dunno, sir. Think he banged his head on something.'

'That boy would do anything to get out of Games!' Rice would say, glaring down at my unmoving number thirteen. 'Well, I suppose someone had better call an ambulance!'

My parents heard about Ryan the same evening via some parent they knew. When Mum asked me for details I told her Ryan had banged his head while larking about near the goal, and she said, 'You boys,' and shoved my football gear in the washing machine like she hated it as much as I did.

That night I even dreamed of Ryan. Dreamed that I woke up and he was standing in the dark at the end of my bed. I was a bit worried at first, but then I remembered that dreams aren't real. Anything can happen in a dream, but nothing can actually hurt you.

'Can't scare me, Bry-Ry,' I said over a fat bit of duvet. 'Push off, go on, scoot back to nightmare land.'

He didn't say a word or make a sound, but his eyes seemed to glow a bit in the dark, which isn't the kind of thing I like to see in my bedroom at night, even in dreams. When his eyes did that I thought, *Hey, what if this isn't a dream?* To make sure I decided to pinch myself. Everyone knows that if you pinch yourself and feel it you're not dreaming, just as if you pinch yourself and don't feel it, you are.

So I sat up in bed and pinched my arm.

And felt it.

That worried me for a sec, but then Ryan

57

vanished, and I thought, *Well, got rid of him anyway*. But then I started to worry about feeling the pinch. If feeling the pinch meant I was awake, what I'd seen at the end of my bed had been real. I certainly felt awake. But then I remembered that in dreams you usually do feel awake, even though you're not. I mean, how often do you say in a dream, 'This doesn't feel real, I must be dreaming'? Not so often.

But that got me thinking. Suppose I'd dreamed feeling the pinch? Who says you can't dream that a pinch hurts? How do we know the person who made that idea famous wasn't someone who didn't feel their own pinch in a dream and wrote a book about it? If it was just one person's experience, maybe other persons, really sensitive super-intelligent persons, *can* feel dream pinches. If that was the case it would mean that I could have dreamt Ryan's visit even *though* I'd felt the pinch.

That thought helped me get back to sleep.

Or dream I went back to sleep.

Chapter Six

I thought of pulling a sickie next day, but I've done that so often over the long years of my school life that even my mother doesn't believe me any more. One day she'll pack me off to school, all pale and droopy and clutching my stomach, and I'll collapse over my desk. Then she'll be sorry.

So I went to school as usual that day. Not in the superhero pantaloons, though. Fished my old ones out of the washing basket. They whiffed a bit because they'd been bundled up all night with one of Dad's sweaty T-shirts and some of his gorgonzola socks, but I could live with that if my class could. At least I could sit down at my desk.

I met Pete and Angie in the street. 'Hey, it's the J-Man!' Pete said, dropping his school bag so he could stand there with his fists on his hips and flash his manky teeth.

'And P-Boy,' I snarled, which burst his bubble right away. 'Heard anything about Ryan?' I asked as we set off for school.

'Like what?' Angie said.

'Well, like if he's still alive.'

'No. How would we?'

We called out to a few others on the way. Most of them hadn't heard anything either, but then we met Julia Frame, who said her mum had found out from Ryan's mum that the hospital described his condition as 'satisfactory'.

'Satisfactory,' I said. 'That's good, isn't it?'

'Depends if you want him to live or not,' said Pete.

It was weird, going through the school gates that day. Kids eyed me every step of the way. Even put their illegal phone chats on hold to stare at me as I went by. I kept my head down. Didn't speak to a soul.

At registration, Mr Dakin told us that our next stop was to be the main hall for a Special Assembly. Oh joy! But at least it would eat in to some lesson time. We strolled to the hall along with the rest of the school, all coming from different direction, slammed through the two sets of double doors, scraped the chairs as loudly as possible as we jostled for seats. Most of the teaching staff were there, also on chairs but up on the stage so they could look down at us and feel superior.

When we'd finally been shouted into silence – Mr Rice did this because he's so good at it – Mr Hubbard stood up and said 'Good morning, everyone!' A dozen whiney little voices said 'G'morning, Mr Huuuubbard,' but the rest of us either kept our traps shut or rumbled. Rumbling's a good thing to do in Assembly. What happens is, you all make this 'errrrrr' sound in the back of your throat and make it go on and on until the person trying to make themselves heard from the stage clears *his* throat to make you stop.

'I've called this Special Assembly,' Mr Hubbard said when he thought he'd got our full attention (the man's mad), 'because of a certain event that I must discuss with you all. As I'm sure you're aware, one of our pupils had an accident during Games yesterday and is now in the district hospital. The young man is unconscious but in a stable condition, and the doctors inform me that he may, unfortunately, remain so for some time. I can

61

give you no more details at present, but this is a very worrying event. How it happened is not clear, though I believe there was no malicious intent on anyone's part...'

He paused to give every eye behind me a chance to burrow into the back of my neck, and everyone in front a chance to turn round and clock me, and everyone on either side of me a chance to bend their necks and take a decko at the person they thought had put Ryan in hospital. When he was satisfied that I would never lift my eyes from the floor again, he carried on.

'I know that many of you will be eager to send Get Well cards to Bryan, but in order to prevent the hospital being deluged with good wishes I have asked all form tutors to organise a card from each class. There'll be ample opportunity during the day for all of you to sign your form cards. At this time, I must ask you to refrain from taking personal gifts and flowers to the hospital. Time enough for that when the patient is sitting up and able to appreciate such gestures.'

'Yeah, like he'll read the cards while he's blanked out,' Pete whispered to me.

Mr Hubbard changed the subject. 'While we're all here,' he said, breaking into a terrifying grin, 'I want to take the opportunity to mention two other, rather more agreeable subjects. Firstly, it's my pleasure to inform you that from next Monday my deputy, Mizz Weeks, will also be absent from school. All being well, before very long she'll be presented with a bouncing baby boy, who, if he's very lucky, in a handful of years will be sitting where you're sitting now, in Ranting Lane uniform, listening to me waffling on from up here.'

He obviously thought 'waffling on' would get a laugh, and it did, from the same creepos who'd said 'G'morning, Mr Huuuubbard'. The rest of us gave a groan of sympathy for the poor kid.

'I'm sure,' Mother H added, 'that you'll join me in wishing Mizz Weeks the very best of confinements, and look forward to her *eventual* return.'

He put his hands together and started clapping, which was a signal for everyone else to clap too. Most of us slapped our palms a couple of times. There were even a few shouts like 'Happy birth, Miss!' and 'If you got any sense you won't come back!', and some of those shrieky two finger whistles I wish I could do. The teachers applauded too. Even the always miserable ones tried to look happy for Miss Weeks. The only one of them who looked uncomfortable was Mr Rice, who'd turned the colour of his tracksuit. No prizes for guessing why. He and Miss Weeks had often been spotted jogging together out of school.

'Finally,' Mr H said when the noise had died and Miss Weeks' ear-to-ear grin had shrunk to normal mouth width, 'I want to remind you that tomorrow is Sponsored Baldness for Charity Day.'

As if we could forget. He'd been banging on about it for weeks. There were posters all over the school, there'd been notes to parents, there'd even been something about it in the local paper. The idea of Sponsored Baldness for Charity Day was that kids who wanted to raise money for some charity to do with heads would shave theirs in time for Friday lessons.

'I'm looking forward to that,' Pete whispered.

'Yeah,' I whispered back. 'Can't wait to see all those hairless skulls.'

'Long as it's not just us, eh?' he replied with a big grin.

'Us?'

His grin dipped a bit. 'You are doing it too, aren't you?'

'Oh sure,' I said, giving him a you-have-to-be-joking smirk. 'Try and stop me.'

Chapter Seven

It wasn't until after lunch, in Food Technology – just the lesson you don't need right after you've eaten – that one of those things happened. The sort of thing that when it's over you can only stare at yourself in the mirror and watch your lips move silently as they try to say, 'Uuuuuuh?'

Kids I know from other schools have been wearing aprons once a week for years, but I'm pleased to report that cooking has been pretty low on the Ranting Lane curriculum all the time I've been there. So low that we'd only had two lessons before this one. In the first we'd been shown how to make an omelette. Mistake. Asking for trouble. Eggs dropped on the counters, the floor, down the back of Skinner's shirt after he snitched on someone for lobbing one at the wall. The second lesson hadn't gone that well either, because when the teacher said, 'Today we're going to make a shepherd's pie,' we wanted to know why the shepherd couldn't make his own rotten pie, and wouldn't let it go for half the period, so there wasn't time to do much.

Mr Bakelite took us for this lesson. Mr Bakelite was a supply teacher, filling in for one of the regulars who'd taken a few months off to get his nerves back into shape. He didn't look all that much older than us. He had this wispy little ginger moustache and tried to be serious and grown up, but it was hard not to see him in school uniform. When he introduced himself to us on day one, some of us looked at others of us. 'We could have fun with this one,' the look said. We did too.

Mr B was a pushover. He'd spent much more time being a kid than in charge of a roomful of them, and he hadn't learnt how to make us be quiet or anything yet. It was so easy to distract him or send him flying up a blind alley. A good example was the way we handled the third cookery lesson. He'd decided to show us how to make a lemon meringue pie, which raised even more eyebrows than the shepherd's pie and the omelette because none of us, boys or girls, could imagine *ever* making a lemon meringue pie except as a lesson.

'You never know when you might be called on to make one for the family,' Mr Bakelite said when Sami Safadi mentioned this.

'For our mums and dads and brothers and sisters?' Sami replied. 'You should visit our planet sometime, sir.'

'I mean for your wives, husbands and children,' said Mr Bakelite. 'And partners.'

'We haven't got any wives, husbands, children and partners.'

'No, but you might have one day.'

'Anyway, you can buy lemon meringue pies at the supermarket,' said Holly Gilder. 'We had one a few months ago. I threw up all over the tablecloth.'

'That was a shop-bought one,' said Mr B. 'Ours will be—'

'I'm allergic to lemon,' said Majid Aziz.

'I can't stand meringue,' said someone else.

'I get spots if something's too sweet,' Trevor Fisher said. 'Is this thing very sweet, sir?'

'Well, it is on the sweet side, but–'

'Cos if it is, I might as well not make it.'

'We're all making it today, Terry, whether we–'

'Trevor, sir.'

'Trevor. We're all–'

'What'll happen to them if we don't want to take them home?' Milo Dakin asked.

'Why wouldn't you take your efforts home?' Mr Bakelite said.

'It'll only be me that eats it. My dad won't. He doesn't like anything unless he's made it, or told me to, or put it on a shopping list.'

'His dad's Mr Dakin,' I said. 'You know Mr Dakin, sir?'

'Yes, I know Mr Dakin, Joseph, but I'm sure–'

'Jiggy,' I said.

'What?'

'My handle. Ignore what it says in the register. It's not spelt J.O.S.E.P.H, it's spelt J.I.G.G.Y. OK?'

'Are you married, sir?' Gemma Kausa asked.

'Married?' Mr B said. 'No. No, I'm afraid not.'

'Why are you afraid, sir?'

'I'm not afraid of anything, I just–'

'Not afraid of *anything*?' said Ian Pitwell. 'Wow!

I'm afraid of charging rhinoceroses, and I don't care who knows it.'

'Have you got a girlfriend, Mr Bakelite?'

'Look, I don't think we need to—'

'Come on, sir, we won't put it in the school newspaper.'

'Is there a school newspaper?' Mr B asked.

'No, but we wouldn't put it in if there was.'

'What's her name, sir?' Hislop wanted to know.

'Whose name?'

'The girlfriend. Does she live with you?'

'I haven't got a girlfriend.'

'Who're you living with then?' someone else asked.

'I'm not living with anyone. I live alone.'

'Oh, that's sad,' said Angie.

'Any kids, sir?' Dob Hegarty asked.

'No. Now listen all of you, nice as it is to chat, we must get on or we'll do *nothing* today.'

We settled down and kindly let him tell us about the ingredients for lemon meringue pie. We knew from the week before what we were supposed to bring in, but most of us hadn't brought anything. He must have expected this because he had a batch of ingredients all ready for us. Not such a good move really, because the ones who'd gone to the trouble of bringing stuff complained that they needn't have bothered. Once the fuss had fizzled, he told us that to save time he'd personally made enough pastry cases for all of us if we shared. 'And last week's list did *not* include ingredients for pastry,' he said when the moans started again. 'I'm providing these pastry cases to speed things up, so all we have to concentrate on today is– '

'Did you make them in your own kitchen, sir, or did you get your secret girlfriend to make them?'

'I told you, I don't have a girlfriend. And yes, I made them in my own kitchen. Now–'

'Is your kitchen in a house, sir?'

'A house? No. I have a flat, but–'

'Is it a big flat?'

'No, not very, it's a bachelor flat. Room for just one person and a swinging cat.'

'Oh, have you got a cat, sir?'

'No, I haven't got a cat, that was just an expression – "there's only room to swing a cat".'

'We've got a cat. It's about the colour of your hair. His name's Ginger. Anyone ever call you that, sir?'

'Not recently. Now let us *please* move on.'

'Got any hobbies, sir?'

'Hobbies?'

'Yeah. Seeing as you ent got a girlfriend.'

'Well, I...yes, I suppose you could call it a hobby. I'm quite an enthusiastic bell-ringer.'

'Bell-ringer? Hey, Atkins is one of those!'

'Atkins? Which is Atkins?' Fingers pointed. Mr Bakelite turned to Eejit Atkins. 'You go bell-ringing, do you?'

Eejit grinned. 'Yer. Fun, bell-ringin'.'

Mr B agreed. 'It's a very rewarding pastime. I'm delighted to hear that a young person from this school enjoys it. What's your first name?'

'Ralph.'

'But everyone calls him Eejit,' I informed him.

'Which bells do you ring, Ralph?' Mr B asked him.

'Not fussy,' Atkins said.

'I mean which church's?'

'Which church's? I don't do many churches.

Not many of 'em has bells, I've looked. Nah, it's houses mostly.'

'Houses?'

'I sneaks up to the door, jams me thumb on the bell, and gets me bum outta there before they comes to see oo it is. One night I did sixty-three. That's me record. I'm thinkin' of startin' on knockers soon. Door knockers, I mean.'

Mr Bakelite turned slowly to the rest of the class. 'What do you say we get back to our lesson?'

So we did. For about twenty seconds before the next round.

'Must have taken you ages to do all these pastry cases, sir.'

'It did take a while.' He looked a bit tired all of a sudden. All that late cooking, probably.

'Do they pay you?'

'Does who pay me?'

'Whoever pays teachers. The education honchos. The school.'

'If you mean was I reimbursed for the ingredients and my time, I can't say I thought about it.'

'So you did it for free?'

73

'Well…yes. But it was my choice, I didn't have to.'

'How much do you get paid, sir?'

'I've just told you, I didn't expect anything for baking these.'

'No, I mean to teach us.'

'I don't really think that's relevant. Now can we just—'

'My dad says teachers are overpaid,' said Wapshott.

'Oh. Well. It's an opinion.'

'That's because his dad sleeps in doorways,' said Nafeesa Aslam.

'He does not!' Wapshott said fiercely. 'He's got a room now!'

'Let us get *on* here!' Mr Bakelite said, quite firmly for him.

It worked, because we let him alone for several minutes this time.

We had to do the cooking in twos, and Pete and I chose each other. We almost always choose each other unless we have to do something in mixed pairs, then one of us usually chooses Angie. Because we don't like teachers looking at us while we're doing stuff we bagged a work counter in a corner, facing the wall. Less chance of getting into trouble if we're not seen.

First off, we had to make the pie filling. This meant spooning cornflour and caster sugar into a bowl, mixing it into an unbumpy paste with water, boiling some more water and some grated lemon rind in a saucepan, mixing the boiled lemony water with the cornflour and sugar paste, boiling *it* up, and simmering the whole lot for a minute, stirring all the time.*

Next we had to mix some lemon juice, beaten egg yolks and butter. After the Great Omelette Disaster, you'd think Mr B would never have given us anything to do with eggs again, but he was safe enough. We'd done that. No point making the same mess twice. We had an egg each. Pete's yolk broke, so he had to ask for another, but mine was perfect. Maybe I'll be a celebrity chef when I leave school.

Once we'd poured the warm yellow filling into the pastry cases we moved on to the meringue topping, which meant whisking the separated egg whites with sugar until we got stiff little peaks. We'd got to the stiff little peaks stage when Pete

* I hope you're getting this down. You never know when some relative or total stranger will order you to make a lemon meringue pie.

asked if he could be excused. 'Excused from what?' Mr Bakelite said. We thought this was his attempt at a joke, but it wasn't, he just wasn't used to being asked to excuse people. Pete explained that he needed to go to the toilet, and Mr B said, 'All right, but hurry back please.'

'And wash your stinking hands, Garrett!' I bawled as he headed for the door. 'This is *food* we're dealing with here!'

While he was gone I started spreading the meringue on our filling – not too neatly because I wanted to keep some of those neat little peaks (which reminded me of a snowy mountain range). I was nearly finished when I felt an itch in my ankle. I scratched the itch and went back to my peaks. I'd got them just the way I wanted when they started moving. I mean waving about. I laughed. What was this, some sort of chemical reaction between egg white and lemon? I looked at the pies some of the others were making. No one else's topping was moving.

'Hey, look at my meringue!' I cried.

A few heads turned, but a heartbeat before their eyes focussed my little peaks froze. Because nothing was happening when the others looked, it must have seemed like I thought I was doing a really terrific job. Milo Dakin, working nearby with this new boy, Harry Potter (poor kid, he goes through hell), said, 'What do you want, Jig, applause?'

Everyone went back to their own toppings – and my little peaks started waving around once more.

I just stared. Helplessly.

I was still staring when the pointy ends of the peaks started snapping off and jumping in the air. That was amazing enough, but then I saw something even more amazing. When the pointy ends snapped off, the peaks grew new ones. I'd never seen anything like it. Wished Pete was there. He wouldn't know what to say about it any more than I did, but at least there'd be someone to share it with.

I heard the door open. Looked round. Pete, right on cue.

It was while my back was turned that the meringue really started jumping. Over my shoulders it went, little bits at first, then bigger bits, bigger and bigger, real lumps, higher and wider all the time until they were splatting the walls, the ceiling, everything that moved or didn't move. Everyone was shouting and trying to dodge the flying meringue.

I flipped back to the pie and got a faceful for my trouble. Clawing meringue out of my eyes I saw that in spite of all the topping that had flown off – much more than we'd made – there was still the same amount as before. If this went on, the room would eventually be so full of lemon meringue that no one would be able to move, yell, or find the door.

Something had to be done. The pie had to be got rid of.

The meringue went even more wild as I reached for it, like it knew what I had in mind and didn't like it. I turned with the pie in my hands. Someone saw me, got it wrong about what I planned to do, and screamed 'You nut, McCue!' I ran to the nearest window, flipped the catch with one hand, and tossed the pie. I didn't watch it go, but of course – of course! – there was a shout from below seconds after I threw it. I leant over the window sill. Mr Rice was looking up at me with a lemon meringue hat on his head.

'McCue! It had to be, didn't it! You'd better have a very good explanation for this, my lad! A *helluvan* explanation!'

He lumbered to the door that would bring him up to our floor.

While Mr Rice was on his way I discovered that everyone in the room thought it was me who'd made all the mess. Even Angie thought it, while Pete marched up to me, meringue running down his shirt, and twisted my wrist. As for Mr Rice...

'Did you do *all* this, McCue?!' he roared when he charged in and saw lemon meringue on everything, everyone.

'I didn't do any of it,' I replied, knowing that I might as well stick my hands up and let him rush me out and lynch me.

'What is the *matter* with you these days, lad?! First you send a boy to hospital–'

'Didn't do that either.'

'–then you go mad in...what lesson is this?!'

'Fodder Technology.'

'What?!'

'Cookery.'

He noticed the ovens, the bowls, the whisks, his ace footie squad in aprons. His lip curled.

'Well even in *Cookery*,' he said, jerking back to me, 'there's no justification for creating such havoc! I'm sure Mr...what's your name?!' he snapped at Mr Bakelite like he was one of the lesser mortals sometimes called students.

Mr B cleared his throat nervously. 'Bakelite. Clive.'

'I'm sure Mr Ballykite-Clive won't mind me handing you notice of detention! Collect the note to your parents from the staff room at the end of the afternoon!'

'Detention for when?' I asked.

'Tomorrow!' he bellowed.

I shook my head. 'Can't do tomorrow.'

'What?!'

'Even if I was guilty and deserved it, which I'm not and don't, tomorrow's already booked.'

'Booked?! For what?!'

'Another detention.'

The Rice orbs turned to pinholes. He leant over me from his great height, forcing me to swing my neck right back on its hinge to return his loving gaze.

A blob of lemon meringue dropped from his hair on to my cheek. I left it there. Sign of weakness to wipe lemon meringue off your cheek when a gorilla in a red tracksuit wants your sweetmeats for a kebab.

'Well, *aren't* we doing well this week, McCue! Whose detention?!'

'Mr Dakin's. Not just me, though, the whole class. Not our fault either.'

'Oh, it never is, is it! Little angels, the lot of you!' He hoofed it to the door. Yanked the door handle. 'Mr Badminton-Clarence, I suggest the *culprit* clears this room up – solo!'

When he'd gone I picked the lemon meringue blob off my cheek and popped it into my mouth. Pretty good, in spite of having travelled all the way up from the playground on hair oil.

'But sir,' I said when Mr Bakelite followed the red twizzler's hint about making me clear up the mess on my lonesome, 'I'll miss Geography.'

'You like Geography, do you, Joseph?'

'Jiggy. Yeah, love it rigid.'

'In that case, consider this a punishment.'

'I might get another detention for not being there.'

'Who's your Geography teacher?'

'Mrs Porterhouse.'

'I'll ask her to excuse you. While I do so, you will stay here and make this room absolutely shipshape – is that understood?'

I hung my head to hide my grin. 'Sir.'

When Mr B turned away, Pete said: 'Jammy devil.'

'Jammy? What for?'

'Getting out of Geography.'

I tapped the side of my head. 'Either got it or you haven't, my son.'

Mr Bakelite dismissed everyone but me early so they could swab themselves down in the toilets. Said he'd cook the pies for them to pick up at home-time.

Only Angie hung back while the rest charged out.

'What was that all about?' she asked me.

'All what?'

'The meringue chucking.'

'No idea, nothing to do with me.'

'Oh, come on. You were the only one near the pie it all came from.'

'Still didn't chuck it.'

82

'So who did, the spirit of some old school cook who thought we were doing it wrong?'

'You tell me.'

She leant close. 'Jig. It's me. Ange.'

'Hey,' I said. 'Thought I recognised you.'

'Tell me what happened. The truth now.'

'The truth? Well OK. If you're sure.'

'I'm sure.'

'Lend me your ear then.'

She stuck her ear out. I put my mouth to it.

'The pie,' I said slowly, 'chucked...*itself*!'

She pulled her ear away.

'You really expect me to believe that?'

'Be nice if you did.'

'Why should I? One good reason.'

'How about we've been friends since birth?'

'Another reason.'

'Because I'm telling you?'

'One more.'

'OK.' I took a breath. Time for the big one. 'One for all,' I said, very seriously, 'and all for lunch.'*

She snorted. 'Don't push it,' she said, and would have flounced after the others if I hadn't grabbed her arm.

---

* That's our motto. Because we're Musketeers, whenever Angie, Pete or I say 'One for all and all for lunch' we have to band together and help one another and believe what whoever says it says.

'Ange.'

She looked at my hand like she'd break it finger by finger if I didn't take it back. I took it back.

'Honest,' I said. 'It wasn't me.'

'The pie threw itself,' she said in a flat voice.

'Come along there please,' said Mr Bakelite in a trying-not-to-sound-stressed voice.

'It did,' I whispered to Angie. 'I was standing there minding my own biz, and it started throwing itself all over the place.'

'Without your help.'

'Without my help.'

'Now why would it do that? *How* would it do that? And why just yours? No one else's pie went doolally.'

'Of course no one else's did. Their names aren't McCue. Their lives haven't been jinxed from the cradle.'

'Come on, we're *done* here!' Mr Bakelite said, keen to clear the room of everyone except me.

'Talk to you later,' I said to Ange as she went.

'Don't count on it,' she replied over her shoulder.

When everyone had gone Mr B tried to give me a lecture about misbehaving and making such a mess, but he hadn't done much lecturing before so he didn't impress me much. I kept saying, 'But sir,' and he kept raising his voice to drown me out, and in the end we both gave up, he left, and I started clearing up the mess I hadn't made.

Chapter Eight

Angie was a bit friendlier at home-time, maybe because she was carrying her half of the perfect lemon meringue pie she'd made with Fiala Kolinski, whose dad's a chef. But not Pete. Pete would have gone home on his own if Ange hadn't gripped his arm with her free hand and marched him between us. That didn't stop him moaning every step of the way, though, which must have got on her nerves as much as mine because eventually she stopped, stood in front of him, and told him to be nice or be smacked.

'Nice?' he said. 'To someone who ruined my lemon meringue pie?'

'*Our* lemon meringue pie,' I reminded him. 'And is that all you're disjointed about? That our pie got spoilt?'

He screwed his face up. 'No, it's not all I'm disjointed about. I'm also disjointed about you covering me with it — me and everyone else, including Mr Bakelite — and *still* getting out of Geography, which I had to sit through bored out of my bedsocks.'

'If I swear to you on my cat's life that I had nothing to do with what that pie did,' I said, 'will you believe me?'

'No,' he said, and pushed past me.

'Garrett!' This was Angie. He was just a few metres along when she spake. He stopped. When the Mint says your name that way you don't keep walking.

'What?'

'Doesn't it occur to you that we've been here before?'

'Occur to me? We come this way most days after school.'

'I mean not believing Jig when he tells us something unbelievable.'

'Oh, that. Yeah, well, doesn't mean he's not spinning one this time.'

'No, but you ought to hear him out, then decide.'

'Don't want to.'

'Why not?'

'He threw my pie round the room and got out of Geography.'

He walked on.

'Garrett!'

This time he didn't stop, even for her.

'Let him go,' I said. 'At least you believe me. One out of two's better than none out of two.'

'Me, believe you?' she said, setting off after Pete. 'Where'd you get that idea? I'm just trying to be fair in the unlikely event that you're *not* telling a porkie.'

I thought of scurrying after her and begging her to believe me, but I was suddenly filled with a very great sorrow. After all we'd been through together my two best friends in all the world wouldn't take my word when I told them something a bit out of the ordinary. Well, if that was how they felt they could do the other thing. I didn't need them. Didn't need anyone.

As I trudged home I tried to put Pete and Angie's disloyalty out of my mind. Distracted myself by trying to work out what the lemon meringue flingfest had been about. I came up empty. No reason, no explanation, no nothing, and in the end did the only thing left. Shrugged it off as one of those unnatural things that happen to me and no one else.

Another person I put out of my mind along with Pete and Angie was Ryan – until that evening as I was sitting down with my parents to pick at a Vegetarian Family Lasagne from the microwave.

'Like what?' I said when Mum asked me if I'd heard anything about him.

'Well, like how he's getting on at the hospital.'

'No.'

'You must have heard something at school.'

'No.'

'Nothing at all?'

I stabbed my lasagne with my fork. 'No!'

I imagined her eyes and dad's eyes meeting over my head, but they could meet as much as they liked. I didn't want to talk about Ryan and that was it. Mum seemed to get this because she let the subject drop. For a while.

'Is that all you're eating?' she asked when I put my fork down after swallowing as much of the stuff on my plate as I could without gagging.

'Had enough.'

'Jiggy, have you been snacking again?'

'No,' I said, though I had, naturally. Who doesn't after school?

'That's not much of a meal.'

'I know, that's why I'm leaving it.'

'What do you mean?'

'It's disgusting.'

'Disgusting? You don't know good food when it's put in front of you.'

'I do, and this isn't it. It's out of a packet from SmartSave, practically glowing with microwaves. I bet it would take you all night to read the additives.'

She turned to Dad, who'd also shoved most of his meal to the side of his plate.

'Don't tell me you don't like it either.'

'All right,' he said.

'Don't you then?'

'Well since you ask, it reminds me of a cow pat.'

Mum threw her knife and fork down.

'Nothing's ever right for you two, is it?'

Dad and I sat quiet. We have to be careful when she's that touchy or she'll pick on one of us for something else. Which she did anyway.

'Jiggy, if you've finished put your knife and fork together.'

'They are together,' I said.

'They're not touching.'

'Why do they have to touch?'

'It's the way they should be placed when you finish eating. You know this. It's the way you've been brought up.'

'I don't see the difference. I also don't see why I have to use a knife for lasagne. There's nothing to cut.'

'Just *do* it, please.'

Maybe I ought to mention this thing my mother has about stuff being perfect. Dad says she's a compulsive-obsessive. Someone who has to have everything just right or they can't rest. He's not wrong about that. You should see her if something gets messed up or broken. Last Christmas is a good example. At Christmas everything has to be totally organised – her way. For instance, she won't let Dad and me decorate the tree or put any decorations up unless she's standing there telling us exactly how to do it, what colours to use, where things have to hang and all. We call her the Christmas Nazi. Last Xmas Day, just before the three of us tucked into the big steaming dinner she'd told Dad and me how to cook (she refuses to cook that day, it's one of her traditions, just sits on a stool giving orders) we pulled three crackers. That's one between her and Dad, one between her and me, and one between me and Dad. The first two had been done – a plastic magnifying glass from the first, a rubber bookmark with a frog's face from the second – and it was time for the third. Dad and I were on opposite sides of the table, so we reached across to pull our cracker, and when it tore apart with a bang this mini screwdriver set jumped out and took a bite out of Mum's wine glass. Red wine all over the snow-white tablecloth she'd set out specially. She was on her feet right away, running for the roll of kitchen towel, then dab-dab-dabbing at the cloth, wailing about it the whole time, while Dad and I sat trying to look sympathetic and sorry. Dad wore a blue paper crown on his head. I wasn't wearing a crown. Mine was still rolled up inside an elastic band – in the gravy boat. It wasn't the stain on the cloth that upset Mum most, though. It was the broken wine glass.

'There are only five left now!' she said as if the ceiling of one of our rooms had caved in.

'Five's enough,' said Dad. 'Only you and I use them.'

'But five's an odd number!' she cried.

'So's three,' he said with a wink at me, 'but we're not having another little McCue just to even things up.'

'I have to have six glasses!'

'No you don't,' Dad said. 'Five's fine.' He started to get up. 'I'll fetch another.'

'Stay where you are! I'll do without!'

He sat down again. Mum put the kitchen roll on the floor – neatly – but we knew from her expression that she wasn't with us any more.

'I'll go to Turpin's for one tomorrow,' she murmured to herself. 'They're bound to be open. Most of the shops will be. I just hope this design's still about.' This got her worrying again. 'Suppose it isn't? Suppose there are no more like this? Oh, I won't sleep tonight!'

Dad raised his half-full wine glass. 'Happy Christmas,' he said.

I raised my half empty cola glass. 'Happy Christmas.'

Mum raised her broken glass with just a drop left in it. 'Happy Christmas,' she said gloomily, and put it down again.

But that was Christmas. The evening of the lemon meringue pie splat, Mum was clearing the tea things away when she started something I would happily have missed.

'Have you thought of going to see your friend?' she said to me.

'Friend? What friend?'

'Ryan. In hospital.'

'See Ryan? Me? In hospital? Why would I do that?'

'Because you were the nearest to him when it happened,' she said, loading the dishwasher. 'And probably the last person he saw before he lost consciousness. Going to see him in hospital would be a nice gesture.'

'I have a gesture for Ryan,' I said, 'and it isn't a nice one.'

'Well, I think you ought to visit him.'

'Think on, Mother,' I said.

'In fact you're going to.'

'I don't think I am.'

'You are. Tonight. Soon as I make the beds, do my face, brush my hair, and put some earrings in.'

'Why have you got to do all that for me to go to the hospital?' I asked. 'Which I'm not doing. Which I wouldn't do if you paid me in solid gold Easter eggs.'

'If I didn't make the beds,' Mum said, rearranging the plates because she'd accidentally put a slightly smaller one between slightly larger ones, 'they never *would* get made, and I have to do the rest because at least one person in this household prefers not to go out looking like something the cat dragged in.'

I eyed Stallone, our cat, who was licking a blob of Vegetarian Family Lasagne off the floor by Mum's feet, but decided not to tell him off for dragging things in. One person being nagged at a time is enough in one house.

'Still don't see why you have to doll yourself up,' I said.

'Well, you can't go on your own,' said Mum.

'They probably wouldn't let you in anyway without an adult.'

'Forget it,' I said. 'I'm not going to see Ryan, with or without you.'

She rammed a little dishwasher tablet in the little dishwasher tablet holder and clicked the door shut. 'Be ready when I come down. Ten minutes.'

'Ten minutes?' I said. 'You, make the beds and give yourself a complete makeover in ten minutes? I don't think so.'

'Twenty at the outside,' she said, shunting out of the kitchen.

'I'm not going,' I said to her back.

'Oh, yes you are,' she said over her shoulder.

'Oh, no I'm not!' I shouted as she went upstairs.

This time she didn't answer.

'You'll go.'

This was Dad. He was still at the table, keeping out of things by quietly reading the boring free local paper that had come through the door during tea. 'Mother has spoken.'

'No chance,' I said. 'This isn't one of those comedy dramas where someone says he's not going to do something at any price and the next scene shows him doing it. It's just not gonna happen.'

'Bet you next week's pocket money.'

I would have taken that bet if the doorbell hadn't gone just then. I went to the front door without being asked because I was in fighting mood and hoped it would be someone I could tell to shove off because we didn't want any. It wasn't someone I could tell to shove off. It was Angie. Pete stood behind her, hands in pockets, looking unhappy.

'What do you want?'

I hadn't forgiven them for the way they'd acted. Angie must have realised this, because she had a freaky little smile on her face.

'One for all and all for lunch?' she said.

I curled my lip. 'Oh, you say that *now*.'

'Pete wants to say it too.' She turned to him. 'Don't you, Pete?'

'Not really,' he grunted.

'Garrett,' she said. 'We've been through this. You *agreed*.'

'You've been through it. You agreed. I'm only here 'cos you threatened to break my legs.'

She pulled him onto the step and stood him

beside her. They looked like they were going to sing carols. Depressing ones. Pete was expected to speak, but he obviously didn't want to. Angie nudged him. He still didn't say anything. She gripped his shoulder and squeezed hard. He winced. Muttered something.

'Speak up!' Ange said sharply.

'One for all and all for lunch,' he said.

I leant forward with an invisible ear trumpet. 'Sorry, didn't quite catch that.'

He screwed his eyes up tight and his mouth twisted like it was having a struggle letting the words through. Finally he spat it out, quite a bit louder this time. 'One for all and all for lunch! OK?'

'It'll do.'

'Great,' said Angie. 'So can we get back to normal now?'

'We can if you swear you believe me about the lemon meringue pie throwing itself about,' I replied.

'We believe you.'

'How do I know?'

'Because I'm *telling* you,' she said through

smiling teeth. 'Now can we come in or have we got to stand out here forever?'

I would have invited them in, and the three of us would have gone up to my room and sprawled and chatted and maybe played some music if we could agree what to put on, but just then two things happened. The first thing was that something furry forced itself between my calves and darted into the garden. This was Stallone, rushing to my mother's rockery to throw up over it. The second thing was my mother coming downstairs.

'You can't have made the beds and done your head already,' I said.

'I decided to just brush my hair. Best get to the hospital sooner rather than later.'

'The hospital?' Angie said.

I chuckled. 'She thinks she's taking me to see Ryan.'

'I think he ought to,' Mum said. 'Besides, the poor lad might be glad of visitors.'

'He's unconscious,' I said. 'But even if he wasn't, he wouldn't want me there. It's a thing the two of us have. It's called hatred.'

'Well, we're going,' she replied in her don't-argue-with-me voice. 'Get your coat.'

I didn't get my coat. I wasn't going and that was final. Or it was until Angie stuck her oar in.

'Can we come?'

Pete and I both said 'Whaaaaaaaat?' together.

'Well, you *can*,' Mum said, 'and welcome, but we don't yet know if he'll be allowed any non-family visitors, let alone four of them.'

'Only one way to find out,' said Ange.

Well, that was it. With her and my mother on the same side I didn't stand a chance. Pete didn't get off either. He made a move away, but Angie hauled him back. It was settled. All four of us were going to the hospital to see Ryan, in our nought-to-sixty-in-half-an-hour car. The only good thing about it was that I hadn't taken Dad's bet.

Chapter Nine

I don't like hospitals at night. Don't like 'em much in the daytime either, but at night, specially when it's dark out, there's this weird feeling about them, like people in head-to-toe bandages could come round corners any minute and shuffle towards you with their arms out. A man in a blue shirt was leaning over a high desk talking to a Golden Oldie in a wheelchair. When we joined them they carried on talking. We stood waiting for them to finish, which meant we couldn't help earwigging their conversation. And what were they talking about? Football. Was there no escape from it? Wherever I go men and boys are talking football. I don't get it. What do they find to say about it? I could dump the subject in nine words. 'Sweaty geezers in shorts kick balls, next subject please.'

'Excuse me,' Mum said, about the time her foot began to tap.

The man leaning over the desk raised a hand like he was stopping traffic, which meant, 'Wait, there's some heavy stuff going down here,' which he really shouldn't have done, because Mum hates being put on hold. On the phone there's not a lot she can do about it, because terrible music kicks in and she's stuck with it. Live, though, in person...

'*Excuse me!*' she said in italics.

The footie chat stopped mid-field. The eyes of the man in the blue shirt and the eyes of the wheelchair-user swerved her way, shocked that she'd interrupted them talking about their religion.

'We're here to visit a patient,' Mum said to the one who wasn't in a wheelchair. 'Are you the person to see?'

'I'm the front desk,' the man said.

He's the front desk. I like that. He's not a man while he's at work, he's a desk. It's like these groups that get together, these committees and all, and the one in charge calls him or herself a chair. Weird. I mean do they have four legs? Do they have a seat for other people to park their rear ends on? Dad says there used to be chairmen and chairwomen, then they became chairpersons, and later still they became just chairs. Evolution. Humans evolving into furniture.

'So how do we get to visit a patient?' Mum asked the man who wanted to be a desk and talk football to people in wheelchairs.

'Which ward are they in?'

'They?'

'The person you're here to see.'

'I don't know. He's a young boy. Had an accident at school.'

'When was he admitted?'

'Yesterday afternoon.'

'Name?'

Mum turned to me. 'What's Ryan's last name?'

'Ryan is his last name.'

'Oh, I always thought... What's his first name then?'

'Dipstick.'

'Jiggy...'

'His first name's Bryan.' It was so difficult to even *say* that.

'Bryan Ryan,' Mum said to the man who wanted to be a desk.

He turned to his monitor and started scrolling slowly down a list. While he was doing this the man in the wheelchair backed up and rolled himself silently away. Maybe he hadn't wanted to talk about football. Maybe football was a sore point for someone who couldn't stand up and he'd been hoping some kind soul would butt in so he could wheel off on the sly.

'There's a Bryan Ryan in ICU,' said the man who wanted to be a desk.

'ICU?'

'The Intensive Care Unit.'

'How do we get there?' Mum asked.

He looked up from the screen to answer, but noticed that his chat buddy wasn't there any more, and frowned instead. If we hadn't come along he'd still have someone to bore the spokes off when he got shot of us.

'I said how do we get there?' Mum repeated sharply.

'Where?'

'The Intensive Care Unit.'

The man who wanted to be a desk made a sound in his throat like he was about to gob at us, and pointed along the corridor.

'End of the corridor, turn right, up the stairs, turn left, see the Intensive Care sign, through the double doors, ring the bell, tell whoever answers it who you want to see, and there you go.'

Mum turned to me, Angie and Pete. 'Did you get all that?'

None of us had. We'd been looking at posters advertising diseases. She asked the man who wanted to be a desk to say it again, and 'More *slowly* please.' He sighed so heavily I thought it was going to be his last, but he managed to go through the directions again, more slowly like he'd been told, and this time we paid attention.

We found our way up the stairs and through the Intensive Care doors, where there was a row of chairs (none of them speaking to committees) and a notice telling us to ring the bell on the wall beside another pair of doors. Mum pressed the bell and after a pause a nurse came out. Mum asked if there was a Bryan Ryan in there. The nurse wanted to know if we were relatives.

'No,' Mum said. 'But these three are classmates of his.'

The nurse wasn't sure about us going in, but a man in a green outfit and white clogs who'd followed her out said he didn't think it would do any harm for us to visit for a few minutes, and the nurse said all right then.

'I'll wait here,' Mum said.

She'd spotted a heap of magazines about hair and plastic surgery. She was already looking through them for ways to improve her hair and face as the nurse led us through the doors.

The nurse called the room a 'bay'. There were just three beds in there, plus her desk. Two of the beds had curtains drawn along the sides. The one that didn't was empty. In one of the occupied beds there was a very fat man with his eyes shut and earpieces in his lugs and a little box on his chest like he was swooning to music.

Ryan was in the other bed. His eyes were shut too, and there was a tube up his nose, and wires stuck to his chest, and a peg sort of thing clamped on the end of one of his fingers. It was horrible. But the thing that most got to me was the screen with the three lines rising and falling and quietly going pip-pip-pip. I couldn't take my eyes off that screen. Couldn't help thinking what if the pip-pip-pips stopped before we left? If that happened I'd get the blame because I was the only one there called McCue. I would have to slide under Ryan's bed before a squad of hospital types came running in to thump his chest or slap him or whatever. If they found me they might make me give him one of my body parts or transfuse some of my blood into him. Ryan and me sharing blood. Neither of us would ever get over that.

The nurse pointed to some chairs and returned to her desk. We placed three of the chairs round the bed. Angie sat on one side, Pete and me on the other. Boys have to stick together, times like that.

'I never saw him like this before,' Pete whispered.

'You mean in pyjamas?' I whispered back. 'With a tube up his snout?'

'I mean so…quiet.'

'That's because he's unconscious,' Angie explained.

'I mean so...still.'

'Unconsciousness kind of does that to a person.'

'Look at that bruise,' I said. You couldn't miss it. It was all over his forehead. 'Proof that I didn't slug him. Only something made of wood could've done that.'

'So maybe you gave *him* a header,' said Pete.

I pointed to my forehead. 'So where's my bruise?'

There were some Get Well cards on the table on Angie's side of the bed. 'From school,' she said, peering at them. She picked one up. 'This is our class's.' She opened it to show me all the signatures. 'Only name missing is the one of the person who put him here.'

I growled. She put the card back. Then we sat wondering what to do next.

'Should have brought some grapes,' Angie said. 'The seedless kind. No worries then about where to spit the pips.'

'He can't eat grapes,' I said. 'Even seedless ones. Look at him.'

'Not for him, for us. I need something to take my mind off being in a hospital.'

'You were the one who wanted to come.'

108

'I thought we ought to.'

'OK, so we're here, what now? We just sit here gazing at him with sad expressions?'

'We could talk to him.'

'Talk to him? What for? He can't answer.'

'They say you should talk to unconscious people,' Angie said.

'You mean as a hobby?'

'In case they can hear.'

'Well, even if he could hear he couldn't answer. If he could answer he wouldn't be unconscious, and if he wasn't unconscious there'd be no need to talk to him in the first place, and we could have stayed at home.'

'Still,' she said, leaning towards the patient. 'How's it going, Bry-Ry?'

Pete chuckled. 'How's it going? How do you think it's going? Look at him. He could be stuffed.'

A thought came to me. 'Hey. For once I can say anything I like to him and even if he can hear he won't come at me swinging his fists. He's just got to lie there and take it.'

Pete liked the sound of that. He smiled for the first time since the last time he smiled. I decided to give it a go. You don't get many opportunities like that with your arch-enemy.

'This'll teach you to keep that rock on your neck to yourself, won't it, Ryan?' I said to him.

He didn't move a muscle. I grinned. This could be fun.

'I don't think we should call him Ryan,' Angie said.

'What else would we call him?' I asked.

'I mean we should use his first name.'

'His first name? Call him Bryan? Get outta here.'

'No, seriously. Seems only right with him like this. It won't be forever. We'll go back to Ryan when he gets conscious again.'

'When he gets conscious again he won't know we were nice to him when he wasn't,' Pete said, 'so why bother?'

'If he can hear,' Angie said, 'calling him by his first name might help bring him out of it.'

'You reckon?' I said.

'It might.'

'In that case...' I leant over the bed. 'Ryan, Ryan, Ryan, Ryan.'

'You're cruel,' said Angie.

'I'm enjoying myself.'

'I never liked Ryan,' Pete said. 'Tosspot. Always was.'

I nodded. 'Hear that, Ryan? You're a tosspot, it's official.'

'A supersize weed,' said Pete.

'A knock-kneed goon,' I said.

'Keep it down,' Angie hissed.

We glanced at the nurse. She looked up and smiled at us. We turned back to Ryan.

'You're a dummy,' I said, quietly.

'A weasel,' said Pete.

'A scumbag,' I said.

'A big girl's blouse,' said Pete.

'Watch it,' hissed Angie.

'You're a wuss,' I said – to Ryan, not Angie.

'You're a prat,' said Pete.

'You're a nit, you're a crumb, you're a big fat bum.'

'A dud. A crud. An old peeled spud.'

'An airhead.'

'A bonehead.'

'A twoodle-woodle.'

'A zeedle-peedle.'

'A monkey up a treedle.'

'Now you're being silly,' said Angie.

'Soup-for-brains,' I said.

'Porridge-for-brains,' said Pete.

'Brain for sale,' I said.

'Who'd buy Ryan's brain?' Pete asked.

'Going cheap,' I said. 'Cheapest brain on the market. Ryan, your brain's about as cheap as a brain can–'

'Oh, very good,' said another voice entirely.

Pete and I – mouths suddenly sewn tight – shipped our eyes up to the face of the nurse who'd joined us while our backs were turned.

'Talking to him's the best thing you can do,' she said. 'There's no telling what he can hear. One more minute now.'

She skipped away, and for the first half of that minute we sat listening to the pip-pip-pip of the this-is-your-life screen. Then I said: 'There is *one* more thing I want to say to him.'

'Must you?' said Angie.

'One last shot while I have the chance.'

I leant close to Ryan, who hadn't blinked, twitched or scratched himself the whole time we'd been there.

'Ryan,' I said. 'You're a *terrible* footballer.'

As it turned out, this wasn't the smartest thing to say, because he must have heard me even in the Land of Nod. Heard and not liked. His eyelids flew up like loose roller blinds. His eyes locked on to mine. His hand (the one without the finger peg) jumped sideways and pinned mine to the covers. I squawked. My chair jerked from under me. As I toppled floorward I felt this zinging sensation like an electric shock from Ryan's hand. The shock zizzered up my arm to my shoulder, then to my neck, and finally to my head, where it buzzed around for a while until his grip went slack. I yanked my hand away and knelt to look up at him. His eyes were closed again.

The nurse was back with us before I'd got to my feet.

'What happened?'

'His eyes opened,' Angie said. 'Made us jump.'

'Sorry,' I said, putting my chair straight.

She wasn't angry with us, though. Not a bit of it.

'You seem to have sparked something in his brain. All that chatter perhaps. It's a good sign.'

'It is?' I said.

'Mm. But I think he's had enough excitement for *one* visit.'

We left. In a hurry. Only just remembered to whip the magazine out of my mother's hands and take her with us.

Chapter Ten

That night I was about as fast asleep as you can get without breaking into a sweat when I felt a presence in my room that jolted me awake. I looked up from my pillow. A dark figure stood looking down at me. I would have screamed for someone to rush in and say 'There, there' while smoothing my hair, but there'd have been no point. The resident Golden Oldies of the McCue household can get all forty of their winks while a hurricane takes the roof off. Mum snores through everything and Dad can't hear a thing because he rams these snore blockers into his earholes.

So there I am in my room, this figure leaning over me in the dark while I don't bother to scream. I bang the pillow over my face, muttering 'It's a dream, it's a dream!' over and over, and when I've convinced myself I peek round and see that he's still there, only he's standing up straight now. I can tell who it is from the outline against the curtains, but in case I have any doubt he tells me, and while he's at it adds a bit more to put the mockers on rest of the night's sleep.

'My name is Bryan Yorick Ryan,' he says in this deadly serious voice, 'soccer star of Ranting Lane, chief head-butter of the Honeybun Estate, fan of the true hero Mr Rice, hospitalised son of a frowning father, unconscious ickle lamb to a doting mother, and I will have my vengeance, in this life or the next.'

Then he fades away.

I fell back on my pillow, trying to get control of my breathing. I knew I hadn't dreamed him this time. That was Ryan all right. Not him in person, but an image of him. His unconscious mind was threatening me from across town, and I had a good idea why. At the hospital I'd said something he couldn't take lying down, even in bed. Something that had jump-started his brain for a few secs while he was plugged in to the mains, jerked his eyelids up and made him squeeze my hand, not in a fond way.

Suddenly I realised what had made the lemon meringue go berserk and get me into trouble in the cookery lesson. Well, not what. Who. Minutes after Ryan headed the goalpost during football practice his unconscious hand had gripped my ankle. He'd been out to get me and I'd thwarted him, but unconsciousness had changed nothing. I felt a sort of tingle where he gripped me, and today, just before the meringue got all peaky, I felt an itch in that same ankle. Maybe that little visit to my room last night and the flying lemon meringue would have been the end of it, but I'd done something unforgivable since then. I'd dissed his ability as a footballer. The latest night visit was to let me know that I wasn't off the hook yet.

Wasn't anything *like* off the hook.

I gulped. If he could make life difficult for me by grabbing my ankle during a nap on a playing field, who knew *what* he might be able to do while wired to the national grid?

Chapter Eleven

Friday morning, last schoolday of the week, yippee. Mum pointed to the kitchen clock, which told me I was running late again, so I grabbed my packed lunch, shouted 'Bye!' to anyone who wanted to hear it, slammed the front door, and trotted across the road to P & A's. Oliver Garrett, Pete's dad, opened the door. He hadn't shaved yet. Looked like a toilet brush with eyes.

'What's this, sleep-walking?' he said. Then he glanced at the top part of my head. 'Couldn't do it, eh? Don't blame you, I wouldn't.'

I would have asked what he meant, but he was already on his way to the kitchen. I dropped my bag and followed him. He climbed back on a high stool at the breakfast bar, where he was half way through his daily plate of sausage, bacon, eggs and tomatoes. Angie's mum's always telling him that stuff like that's bad for you, except maybe the tomatoes, and the only way he's going to get it is if he cooks it himself, which he does. Looked pretty good to me. I'm only allowed porridge or cereal and a slice of toast in the morning. Sometimes a Pop-Tart. Or a waffle. Every now and then a pancake. I have a deprived childhood.

'Park your posterior,' Oliver said round a sausage.

I sat down on one of the chairs at the table that stopped being any use as a table about a month ago. It had been a glass topped table until the big metal lampshade that hung over it crashed down one evening while they had their nosebags on. Angie told me all about it. No warning, she said. The four of them were tucking into a casserole when the shade came down, smashed the glass, charged right through to the floor. All they could do was sit there looking into this sudden pit where the lampshade had gone, taking the casserole dish and their plates with it.

Oliver and I didn't say much to one another. He was reading the paper. I've known him all my life but we don't have many really heavy conversations. Audrey's easier. Audrey's Angie's mum. When she came down a couple of minutes after I arrived she said, 'You're early, Jig.' I said that I didn't think

I was, and she said, 'Well, earlier than usual.'

She went to the foot of the stairs and called Angie and Pete. Angie yelled, 'I'M COMING!' in that nice gentle way she has.

As Aud went round stuffing things into the shoulder bag she takes to work she said, 'Couldn't go through with it, I see.'

'Through with what?'

She tapped the side of her head. I didn't know what she meant but it was too early for joking around, so I just shrugged. Shrugs come in handy sometimes. You can answer all sorts of questions with shrugs. Some people think shoulders are to stop our jackets falling off, but that's wrong. You can always hang your jacket on the back of a chair, but you can't shrug without a shoulder. Teachers aren't big fans of shrugs. I should know. The number of tellings-off I've had for shrugging when one of them asks me something.

Angie came rattling down the stairs and into the kitchen. 'What are you doing here?' she demanded.

'It's a school day.'

'But you're early.'

'Why does everyone keep saying that?'

'Maybe 'cos it's true.'

She looked at the clock on the wall. So did I, first time since I'd come in. She was right, I was early. But how…?

I was still wondering about this when she said: 'Pete won't be very pleased with you.'

'Eh? Why not? What have I done?'

'It's what you haven't done.'

She was eying the top third of my head. And grinning. I didn't grin. Nothing to grin about. I'd just realised why I was so early. My mother must have rigged our kitchen clock to trick me into leaving the house in good time. Right. That was it. She was going into a home as soon as I was old enough to arrange it.

A minute later I realised something else. What all the head talk had been about. This occurred when Pete sloped into the kitchen with a multi-coloured woolly bobble hat pulled down over his ears. It was Sponsored Baldness for Charity Day.

'You haven't,' I said in disbelief.

He scowled. '*You* haven't.'

'Why would I? Why would *anybody*?'

'You said you would.'

'I didn't.'

'You did. Yesterday. I said, "You are doing it too, aren't you?" and you said, "Try and stop me".'

'Pete, I was being sarcastic.'

'Well that's just terrific,' he said. 'That's just dandy. That's the Queen's knickers, that is.'

'You've actually shaved your head?' I said.

'With my razor,' said Oliver on his way out of the kitchen. 'Ran the battery down last night and didn't put it on charge.

'Let's see,' I said to Pete.

'No.'

'Oh, go on.'

'No.'

'Planning on wearing that all day then, are you?'

'Probably.'

'Won't be allowed. Anyway, there'll be plenty of other bald twits there.'

'There'd better be,' Pete said.

The first bald person we met on the way to school was Eejit Atkins.

'Good, innit?' he said when we gaped at his head. 'Me bruvver did it.'

His big brother Jolyon had run a razor all along

122

the top, made a parting as wide as a hand right down to the back of Eejit's skinny little neck, then shaved each side into a square. In each square he'd cut two round bits, and in the middle of each round bit he'd painted a bloodshot eyeball.

'Where's yours then?' Eejit said to me.

'My what?'

'Yer 'ead?'

'It's on me neck, Eej. Just follow the signs.'

'I mean why din't ya shave it orf like me and Garrett?'

'Because I'm not a moron,' I said.

'At's no excuse, you shoulda.'

'Next time.'

'Nex' time?'

'Next time I need my head examined.'

Eejit spotted a couple of also bald mates at the end of the road and scampered after them. We stood watching him go.

'Just me and Atkins and his chimp pals,' Pete wailed. 'What have I done?'

We started walking again.

After a few steps Pete yawned, a full head yawn. 'I'll never get through the day,' he said. 'I was awake all night worrying that I looked stupid.'

'You were right to,' I said.

'It was OK while I was doing it. Had a real laugh as it all came off and blocked the plughole. Laughed myself to sleep even.'

'You said you were awake all night.'

'Most of it. I woke up needing a pee, forgot about being hairless, looked in the bathroom mirror, had the screaming heebies.'

'You woke the whole house,' Angie said.

'Count yourself lucky,' I said. 'No one in my house even *hears* screams.'

'Couldn't get back to sleep after that,' Pete said. 'Tossing and turning till it got light, thinking what if me and Jig were the only ones who did it.' He screwed his face up at me. 'Then you betrayed me.'

'Sorry,' I said.

'And suppose it doesn't grow back?'

'Course it will,' Angie said. 'Grow is what hair does. Usually.'

'Or it grows back curly. Dad said it might. Pity he didn't say it *before* I clipped it. If he'd said it before I'd never've done it.'

'We could call you Curly if it grows back that way,' I said.

'Curly Garrett,' he snarled. 'Yeah, that'd make it so much easier to live with.'

As it turned out, Pete and Eejit's mob weren't the only bald ones. Some of the others wore hats too, either because they weren't used to what wasn't underneath yet or because their mothers had said they must or they'd catch cold. Even Kryss Rosakis had shaved his head for his first day back after his suspension.* Some of the girls had gone bald overnight too, including a couple from our class. 'I don't believe it!' Angie cried when she saw that Julia Frame was one of them.

'She looks like a boiled egg with a face drawn on,' I said.

'What with that and last week,' Angie said, 'that girl's well on the way to making a name for herself.'

'What happened last week?'

'I paid her back for grassing me up to Mr Prior.'

I remembered the day of the grassing. It was in RE about ten days ago. Mr Prior had written a list on the board of these beardy old time religious types under the heading 'Famous Prophets'

---

* The suspension was for asking teachers the kind of lame questions that make them blow their tops, and secretly filming them on his mobile, putting the results on his website. Rosakis also superimposed their heads on sheep and cows, with the caption, 'Do you want your child taught by these animals?' Pretty good, we thought.

and told us to memorise them in ten minutes flat – 'AND NOT MAKE NOTES!' – because he was going to test us when he got back from a smoke. He didn't actually say he was going for a smoke, but every time he returns from somewhere he smells like one of the old brick factory chimneys. While he was gone, Angie went to the board and changed the word Prophets to Puppets which caused a giggle or two, but when Prior came back in a cloud of smoke and demanded to know who'd done it Julia Frame said it was Angie, and he gave Ange detention.

'Where was I when you paid Julia back?' I asked.

'You were off that day. The virus you said you caught from your dad's PC.'

'What did you do to her?'

'She went to Zappa's Jokes in the arcade,' said Pete.

'Zappa's Jokes?' I said to Angie. 'Not your usual sort of shop.'

'No, but I wanted something that would embarrass Julia. Thought Zappa's 'd be the place. I was right.'

126

'What did you get?'

'A Whoopee Remote. Set it off in Mr Hurley's class. Best class to get *anyone* in trouble.'

'What's a Whoopee Remote?'

'You stick this little speaker under someone's chair and when you press a button across the room rude noises go off – under the chair.'

'You did that to Julia?'

'Yeh. Every time Hurley paused.'

I grinned. 'Brilliant!'

'Pretty sad really,' Angie said.

I shredded the grin. 'That's what I meant. Where's this gadget now?'

'Sold it to Eejit Atkins for twice what I paid. His grandma was coming to stay.' She smiled brightly. 'I made a profit *and* got Julia a double detention!'

Chapter Twelve

Sponsored Baldness for Charity Day was the big deal of that Friday. As well as Pete and Julia and Atkins and quite a few others, half a dozen of the male teachers − but not the *Head* − had also nuddified their skulls. One of the half dozen was Mr Prior, but shaving his dome for charity wasn't such a stretch. He'd only had a couple of feathery bits over his ears before. One of the others was the Resistant Materials king, Mr Dent. Mr D never takes himself as seriously as some of them, and as well as losing his mop he'd made a sort of halo out of cardboard, which was balanced on his ears, and the halo had two little arrows standing up on the rim pointing at his head. Pretty neat, I thought.

The only suddenly-bald teacher that really amazed us was Mr Rice. Yes, the Ricipops had shaved his roof! He was a head case even before today, but there he was, standing proudly in the playground in his red tracksuit and shiny nut.

Quite a few mouths dropped open at the sight of him. But there was something extra about Rice's baldness. With his hair gone we could see the tattoo that had been under it all this time. I can't imagine what sort of haircut he must have had when he had it done, but it was on the back of his head, between his ears. It was a heart with the words 'Dotty forever'. That was a surprise. I mean I was surprised that he knew it. But later he told us – because we kept on and on about it and he knew he'd get no peace till he did – that he was eighteen when he had the tattoo done, and Dotty was the name of his girlfriend at the time.

Pete ditched the bobble hat at registration because Face-Ache (who'd kept his hair on for a change) told him to. He didn't seem to feel too bad about this, though, because by then he'd found out that he was just one of eight baldies in class. They all got together during break and talked about not having any hair and what fun it was, even if it was a bit drafty, while those of us still with hair said they were off their heads.

At lunchtime, Ange and I sat on our private bench in the Concrete Garden. Pete usually sits with us at lunch, but at first he was in the playground with the other baldies, all standing together like a bunch of grapes. We were about half done by the time he joined us.

'The mad social whirl,' he said, running a hand over his gleaming northern hemisphere.

I offered him the bag of hamster flavour crisps my mother was trying out on me. He crammed some into his gap, then spat them out again like I'd done when I tasted them.

'Heard your good news,' I said as he swigged my bottle of fruit juice.

'What good news?'

'Results of your dyslexia test.'

He glared at Angie. 'That was a secret.'

'It's only Jig,' she said.

'So you're not dyslexic after all,' I said. 'Just stupid.'

'Watch it, McCue, I have other friends now.'

We munched some more of our crummy packed lunches in silence. I'd spent the morning murdering every nude head joke I could think of, and I was all joked out. Pete's the joker of the Musketeers and he hadn't even made one because he didn't see the funny side. There was one more head joke to come, though, and this one was on him, literally on him, and I was the one to play it.

'Well, he said he didn't sleep much last night,' Angie said about ten minutes before the end of lunch break.

We'd watched Pete's chin sink lower and lower on his chest. His eyes were closed, he was breathing gently. I remembered Mr Rice's tattoo. My fingers twitched towards the felt pen in my pocket.

'Jig, you can't,' Angie whispered.

'I can,' I said. 'Remember my football shirt?'

'He wrote a number on it, that's all. You didn't mind so much.'

'Well maybe he won't mind if I write something on his head then.'

'Like what?'

I printed VACANT on the top of Garrett's nude bonce.

'Is that the best you can do?' Angie said.

'I didn't hear any better ideas from you.'

'You didn't ask for any.'

'What would you have come up with if I had?'

'Something better than that.'

'Like what?'

'Too late, you've done it.'

'Tell me anyway.'

'No.'

'You can't think of anything.'

'I can.'

'All right, let's see you do something better on some other slaphead.'

'There aren't any others that are asleep.'

'You wouldn't do it if there were.'

'I would.'

'What then?'

'Not telling.'

We might have gone on a bit longer like this, but Pete snorted in his sleep like he might wake up any second, so we ran to the corner. If he opened his eyes and we weren't there he couldn't blame us for the word on his head.

Just around the corner we crashed into some girls, older girls, who offered to duff us up for not minding where we went. I would have apologised, but Angie pulled one of her mean faces and invited them to try, and even though she was shorter than them they let us off. Just before we left them I glanced back at Pete. He was still asleep, chin on his chest. The word 'VACANT' on top of his head really caught the light. One of the girls peered round to see what I was looking at. She nudged the others. They were covering their mouths as Ange and I heel-and-toed it.

Chapter Thirteen

With all that Sponsored Baldness for Charity going on, I'd hardly given Ryan a thought all morning, and it was afternoon already, the day was more than half over. Maybe the flying meringue had been the worst his unconscious mind could do, I thought. Yeah, that was it. I was safe. Ryan was out of the picture. All I had to worry about in Mr Hurley's history class was sliding under my desk with boredom.

'Care to share the joke with us, Mr McCue?'

'Sir?'

'Why are you smiling?'

'Just glad to be here with you,' I said truthfully.

'Any more backchat like that,' he snapped, 'and it's detention for you.'

I give up.

The only real worry now was Pete. He hadn't made it to class. Angie caught my eye across the room and tossed it back. One of us mouthed Pete's name and the other one shrugged. I knew what she was thinking. I was thinking it too. That Pete must still be dozing in the Concrete Garden. Mr Hurley had asked me where he was when we came in, probably because he sits next to me at the back (Pete, not Mr Hurley) and I'd said I wasn't sure but that he'd said something about not feeling too well earlier, and Hurley let it go.

I'd been trying to look like I was paying attention in the lesson, but the drawing I was doing inside the back cover of my exercise book was much more interesting. It was of a dead ancient Egyptian having his brain pulled out through his nostrils with a long hook. I like ancient Egyptians. I like their paintings. Like the way they put their mummies in pyramids. Don't know where they put their daddies. Garden sheds, probably.

I was really into my drawing when I noticed that the droning voice of our beloved history teacher seemed quieter than last time I listened. I looked up. He was still down the front, pointing at the latest load of historical haddock he'd chalked on the board for us to copy into our books. Between him and me were the other kids, jaws in palms, trying to keep their eyes open. But some of the kids weren't there any more. The swats down the front still were, but some of the lesser swats along the sides had disappeared, along with their desks. The walls of the room had moved in, and were still moving, and as they moved more kids and desks vanished without a murmur. The ceiling was moving too. Getting lower and lower. Another couple of minutes and there'd be nothing left. No one. I didn't know what to think. Didn't know what to do either, but I had to do something if I didn't want to be squashed or disappeared. There was still a fair bit of space between me and the ceiling, but maybe because it was getting lower all the time I bent my head, and when I bent my head my eyes fell on my drawing.* There was something different about it now. The hook hauling brain out of the ancient Egyptian's hooter wasn't hooking it out of an ancient Egyptian's hooter any more. It was hauling it out of Bryan Ryan's. Whose eyes were open. Staring up at me.

I jumped up with a startled 'Eeeek!' and beetled towards the front, running low like someone doing a commando in Charades. As I got there I heard

* No, I don't mean they fell out, don't be stupid, I mean they *focussed* on it.

Mr Hurley say my name somewhere in the distance, but now wasn't the time to stop for a natter. I swerved near his legs and made it to the door. Fortunately the door had come in with the wall, though the handle was just below the ceiling now. I reached up, feeling kind of like *Alice in Historyland* but without the flowing locks and pinafore. I turned the handle, pulled the door, zipped out into the corridor, where—

The ceiling and walls had also closed in!

From where I crouched, the corridor looked like a secret tunnel, but it was the only way out. I started along it, running in a crouch, aiming for the exit doors at the end. As I ran the ceiling continued to get lower and the walls continued to come in, but I reached the doors in time. They were double doors, much smaller than usual because they'd shrunk with the corridor, but the playground was just the other side of them. All I had to do was push them back and I'd be outside, under lots of lovely grey sky. I pushed the bar on one of the doors. It moved, but the door didn't open. I pushed the bar on the other door. It didn't open either.

Panic.

I looked behind me, under my armpit. The corridor was so low and narrow now that I didn't stand a chance of going back that way. But there was another door, just a few steps in from where I crouched. I backed up. Tried the door. It opened. I hobbled in, knees under my chin, looked around. The walls and ceiling were where they should be! Just one snag. This was a toilet. One of the girls' toilets. Still, at least I could stand upright in here, if not to pee. Funny thing, though. As I rose to my full glorious height I felt a chronic need to sit down. My nerves had got themselves pretty wracked out there. Well, I'd come to the right place for sitting. I lurched into one of the cubicles and parked myself on the seat, probably the first boy to ever sit there. I didn't close the door. If any girls shuffled in I would cry 'Sanctuary!' They couldn't turn me out if I said that.

I shut my eyes, needing to sit quiet and get my breath back. Even when I got it back I kept the old orbs closed. I had some thinking to do, and it's sometimes easier to think when you can't see anything. Specially if you're a boy in a girls' toilet. This was all Ryan's doing, of course.

Somehow, from his hospital bed, he'd made the classroom walls and ceiling close in and turned the corridor into a tunnel. Tunnel. Maybe where he was, where his mind was, he felt like he was in a tunnel with no way out and he wanted me to feel it too.

Pip-pip-pip.

What was that?

Pip-pip-pip-pip-pip-pip.

I opened my eyes. My cubicle had gone. So had all the others. So had the washbasins and mirrors. So had the walls and ceiling. So had the door to the corridor. I was still sitting on the toilet though. But in a desert. A red desert. Nothing to see in any direction but red sand. The sky was reddish too, kind of streaky like running paint, and there was this ultra-white sun that hurt your eyes.

Pip-pip-pip-pip-pip-pip-pip-pip-pip.

Something bothered me about those pips. I'd heard them before somewhere. I got off the toilet. Turned to look at it, don't know why, habit maybe. It wasn't a toilet any more. It was a wooden sign, the kind of sign estate agents use, and there were two words on it. 'To Let'.

Pip-pip-pip-pip-pip-pip-pip-pip-pip-pip-pip-pip-pip.

The pips were getting urgent, like something was wrong.

Then something appeared in front of me, right where the basins had been. A screen, hovering in the air. It was like the screen beside Ryan's hospital bed, and it was where the pips were coming from. All of a sudden I understood. The empty red desert was the inside of Ryan's head, and this was the screen that showed he was still al—

Piiiiiiiiiiiiiiiiiiiiiiiiiiiiiiiiiiiiiiiiiiiiiiiiiiiiiiiiiiiiiiiiiiiii

I started. The pip-pip-pips had become a single pip without a 'p' at the end and the little blips weren't dancing any more. I'd seen enough trailers for TV med shows to know what that meant. When the lines stop pipping and the dancing blips become straight lines, the person in the bed nearest the screen has switched off.

I stepped back with a horrible fear. As I stepped back, the ultra-white sun shrank, went dull, became a lightbulb. The streaky red sky turned back into a cream-coloured ceiling. Walls appeared, and a floor, and the cubicles

140

and basins returned. And the mirrors. And the door. I stumbled to the door. I opened it. Peered out. The corridor wasn't a tunnel any more. It was normal. Kids were mooching along it.

'Oi, McCue, whatchoo doin' in the Girls?' one of them bawled.

I didn't bother to answer. I ran to the exit doors, pushed the bars. The doors opened. I shot outside. I had to get to the hospital right away. Had to find out if Ryan was still alive. Or not.

Chapter Fourteen

The hospital isn't as far from the school as it is from home, specially if you run all the way, so I was there in ten minutes or so. There was a different man at the front desk this time, but I wasn't sure if you had to ask him if you could go any further or what. I decided that maybe I'd better and got behind the two bundles of visitors who were waiting to talk to him as soon as a third bundle had got what they wanted out of him.

There was this big clock on the wall behind the desk, and as it was all there was to look at apart from the disease posters I watched the second hand jerking round, second by second by second. Jerk, jerk, jerk, it went. Jerk, jerk, jerk, endlessly. It was fascinating. Jerk, jerk, jerk. At first. Jerk, jerk, jerk. Not so much after a while though. Jerk, jerk, jerk. It seemed to get slower and slower as I watched – jerk... jeeerk...jeeeeerk... – until my body started to sag, eyelids too, and – jerrrrrrrrrk – I got to thinking that much more of this and I'd either slump to the ground snoring or go stark jerking mad.

I dragged my drooping eyes away from the clock and took in the people waiting in front of me to talk to the man at the desk. The three bundles of visitors were still there, but now there was a fourth bundle as well. The fourth bundle had arrived while I was watching the jerking clock, slotted themselves between the third bundle and me like I didn't exist. I was so hacked off about this that I decided to skip the man at the desk. He couldn't see me anyway behind all those people.

As I zipped along the corridor and up the stairs, my nerves kicked in. What would I find when I got to the ward? By the time I reached the first floor I was jigging so badly that I had to hang back and get my feet and flapping arms under control. When my twitches were down to a minimum I took an ultra-deep breath and went through the double doors to the Intensive Care Unit. I rang the bell beside the second set of double doors. The same nurse as last night came out. Had she been here ever since? She asked if she could help me.

'Um…' I said, wishing Mum was there. I wasn't used to talking to people in hospitals.

'You were here last night, weren't you?' the nurse said. 'Come to see your friend again? Well, I'm afraid…'

My heart almost punched a hole in my chest. She was afraid? Afraid of what? To tell me that Ryan had…?

'Just a minute,' she said then. 'I'll go and see if it's all right for you to go in too.'

I was just going to say, 'No, don't bother, it's all right, really, I'll go away and hide in my room for the rest of eternity,' but before I could get the first word out I was staring at the closed doors again.

She wasn't gone long. 'It's fine,' she said when she swung back through the doors. 'She doesn't mind at all.'

'She?'

'Your friend's poor mother.'

She held one of the doors open for me. I had to go in.

Nothing seemed to have changed in the bay since last night. The third bed was still empty and the fat man was still in the second bed, eyes closed, little box on his chest, earpieces plugged in. It occurred to me as I passed him that maybe it wasn't music he was listening to. Maybe it was some therapist helping him lose weight without doing any exercise.

'Hello!'

This came from the woman sitting by Ryan's bed. Small chunky woman with big blue eyes and hair like pipe cleaners. I knew her by sight. Used to see her at school in the infants, with her little boy, and the juniors for a while when he was bigger. I'd also seen her not so long ago in the doorway of her house on the Honeybun Estate.

'The nurse tells me you're from Bryan's class.'

I moved closer. 'Yes.'

Mrs Ryan smiled sadly at me. 'Oh, he'd be so happy to know that one of his friends had been to see him.'

My thudding heart plunged into my stomach, and from there down one of my legs. 'He'd be so happy to know that one of his friends had been to see him.' That could only mean one thing. She was being very brave while she said goodbye to him before they gave his bed to someone with a pulse.

She was inviting me to look at the body of her dead son!

'Look at his face,' Mrs Ryan said lovingly.

I looked at Ryan's face. His eyes were closed for good now. And he was smiling. His last smile. My arch-enemy would never cause me grief again. I almost burst into tears.

I felt I ought to say something, anything, but the best I could come up with was to ask if Mr Ryan had been to see him.

'He's at the snooker club,' she said. 'He'll be along later.'

I was shocked. She'd come to see the body of their son while her old man played *snooker*?

'Shouldn't you be at school?' she asked while I was still reeling.

'Yes. But I wanted to...you know.'

'See Bryan?'

'Yes.'

She touched my arm. 'Aah.' She looked so grateful. I felt bad. About lying to her. About stepping away from the goalpost. Guilty as sin on all counts.

After that we just gazed at Ryan's smiling face, gazed in silence while I wondered how much longer I'd have to do this before I could make some excuse to leave. They hadn't disconnected him from the gizmos yet. The tube was still up his nose, the wires were still stuck to his chest, the peg was still attached to his finger. Probably waiting for his mum to shove off, I thought. Except...

Plp-plp-plp-plp-plp-plp-plp-plp-plp

My eyes drifted to the screen beside the bed. The three blip lines were jumping along as merrily as ever.

'Um,' I said. 'He's not...?'

'Not what, dear?'

'I mean is he...?'

'Going to come out of it? Well, they can't be sure, but they say the signs are good.'

'They do?'

She gave me a great big beam of a smile.

'He perked up about twenty minutes ago. They called me at work and I came straight round.'

'Perked up?'

'The nurse who was checking him over at the time told me that the screen went wild all of a sudden. Something he was dreaming, she thought. When it settled down this lovely smile crept onto his face, like he... Are you all right, dear? You've gone a funny colour.'

I muttered something about not feeling well and having to get back to school. As I left her, Mrs Ryan called softly after me.

'Thanks for coming. So kind of you. I know Bryan would be very touched.'

I went downstairs in a daze. I didn't know whether to be relieved or hopping mad. On the way to the exit I passed some of the same people as before at the front desk. I would still have been there with them if I hadn't gone up without asking.

I walked to the revolving doors that would take me out of there. There were unrevolving doors too, wide ones for wide people and people in wheelchairs, but I'm not either of those and besides I like revolving doors. I stepped into the nearest open section and gave the glass in front of me a shove. The doors started revolving, as I expected them to, but not as slowly as they should from such a little push. I would have jumped out at the exit, but it went by too soon and I had to go round again – and

148

again – and again – faster and faster all the time as the doors picked up more and more speed. Soon I was running – I mean really racing – to keep ahead of the section behing me. As I hurtled round I glimpsed and glimpsed and glimpsed the desk man coming towards me. The doors slowed as he got closer, slower and slower, and stopped altogether as he arrived. I stood facing him.

'What the devil are you up to?'

I couldn't speak. It took all my strength to keep my head from spinning off my neck.

'Bloody kids. Get out of here, go on, and don't come back!'

As I tottered through one of the swishy non-revolving doors I heard a voice in my head.

Ryan's voice.

'Hey,' it said, 'this vengeance deal is a blast. Now what shall we do *next*...?'

Chapter Fifteen

There was no one in yet when I got home. Just as well or there'd have been questions, like why was I there so early. After I'd gulped some bubbly I sloped up to the spare room to see if I could find something to take my mind off what had just happened – and the fact that Ryan, could still get to me after all, wherever and whenever he liked.

Our spare room's a tip. Crammed floor to ceiling with things nobody has any use for, old games and jigsaw puzzles, blankets and lumpy pillows, radios with dead batteries, boxes of ancient crockery that belonged to Mum's gran, other boxes of who-knows-what. Most of it's junk that wouldn't be missed if the house burned down, but it's all there for a reason. The reason is that there's no room for guests in a room that full. At our old house on Borderline Way, Mum used to get all tense whenever people came to stay. Didn't matter who they were. Guests ruined her routines, her ways of doing things, even forced her to read cookery books. But it wasn't just Mum. Dad and I weren't keen either. When we had visitors we had to watch things on TV that we'd rather not, spend more time sitting together than seemed natural, and everything in the house had to be in just the right place all the time. It was such a strain. Stuffing the spare room in this house was Dad's idea. 'Not only do we not put a bed in there,' he said just after we moved in. 'We make it impossible for one to even *fit* in there.' Mum was a bit iffy about it at first. To her, a room full of junk is like a house of horrors. I was the one who solved that one. 'Don't go in there,' I said to her. 'Never even open the door. Pretend there's no such room.' And that's what she does. And it works. When people ring and suggest spending a weekend or a few days with us, she says, like she really believes it, 'I only wish we had the *room*, but it's just a two-bedroom house,' and Dad and I slap hands silently in the background.

I don't know what I was looking for in the spare room after my trip to the hospital (couldn't even take a wild guest) but after pushing a few things out of the way and tripping over a few others, I saw my old blackboard and easel from when I was little. There was still a bit of a drawing in one corner of the board of a character from a kiddie TV programme about firemen that I used to watch. The easel was bright red and made of metal and only a bit scratched, and someone – Mum obviously – had taped my old box of coloured chalks to it. Suddenly I wanted to use those chalks. I pulled the blackboard and the easel out and carted them to my room.

I have a desk in my room where I do my homework when I really have to, or when I can't get any peace downstairs. I made some space for the easel so the blackboard would be at eye height rather than waist height, and opened the box of chalks. Some of them were broken and some were down to the length of a finger joint, but I shook them out on my desk and tried to decide what to draw. I decided to keep the fragment of old picture of the fireman. It was from my past. I couldn't just rub out my past. I drew a line across the corner to fence it off. That cheery old fireman's face would stay there forever now, as a reminder of the good old days before I started school and my life started going downhill.

I had no idea what to draw, so I just doodled for a while hoping I'd think of something. I didn't want to draw things I see all the time, like houses and trees, but what? A robot? A rocket ship? Someone with his neck in a noose or a dagger in his back? I wasn't in the mood for that sort of thing. I rubbed out my doodle (careful not to touch my kiddie pic of the fireman) and drew a horizontal line. A horizontal line is a good thing to start with quite often because anything can stand on or hang from a horizontal line. The obvious thing was to make it the horizon of the sea, so I started to draw a ship on it. At first it was one of those big old liner types, with funnels and smoke and all, but that was pretty boring, so I rubbed out the funnels and smoke and drew some sails. Then I thought, 'Ah-ha, a pirate ship!' I hadn't drawn a pirate ship for quite a while. Pirate ships are fun. All that rigging, the rope ladders, the Jolly Roger with the skull and crossbones, the pirates looking over the sides and waving cutlasses, and maybe, in the distance, another ship, firing canons, and a canon ball flying at the first ship. Maybe make a hole in the sail where a previous canon ball has already gone because there's a battle going on. Yes!

In about twenty minutes I was really into this. Into the detail. I like detail in drawings. All the itsy-bitsy stuff you have to screw your eyes up to see. Mr Lubelski says that if I did more drawing I could get really good at it, but mostly I don't bother.

Mr Lubelski. I froze. About now I should be on my way with the rest of my class to a quiet hour with Face-Ache Dakin, where we'd have to write over and over something like, 'I must not be late for my stupid Maths lesson.'* Mr Lubelski was the cause of this detention, though I'm sure it wasn't deliberate. He's a nice man but kind of absent-minded, and it was this absent-mindedness that got it for us. In Monday's Art lesson he set us this task while he went to see Mother Hubbard about some materials he'd ordered. The task was to start on a batch of pots and pans he'd arranged specially. Drawing them, I mean, not cleaning them. But he couldn't just leave us, he said, because there'd been a lot of bunking off lately and

* In most detentions we have to complete unfinished work or do homework, but Dakin makes us write lines, which is even more boring. 'Lines were good enough for me when I was at school,' he said once, 'so they're good enough for you.' Mr Hurley is a lines man too. They must have gone to the same school.

the staff had been told not to leave classes unattended, so he locked the door to keep us in. And forgot to come back. By the time someone heard us pounding on the door and we were let out by Mr Heathcliff the caretaker, we were late for Maths with Mr Dakin. Face-Ache isn't good at listening, not to kids anyway, and he gave the whole lot of us detention when we tried to tell him we'd been locked in by a teacher. He wanted to set it for the following night but some of us already had one that night, and others had after-school activities like Chess or Snail Racing, so it had to be put off today, Friday. And here was I at home, drawing pirate ships on my junior blackboard. Oh, well.

I carried on with my drawing when Mum got in from work. I didn't tell her about my second hospital visit, just shouted hello down the stairs when she shouted hello up them. The drawing was really coming to life by then, specially the main pirate ship. I spent ages on the rigging, the vessel, the sea. Kind of wished I'd done it on paper because it wouldn't get smudged on paper, but it was good to use chalk. Messy, but good. Maybe

Mr Hurley feels the same way. He's the only teacher who still uses a blackboard, and boy does he make the most of it. He told us once that he started his teaching life using one and he's going to end it using one. But I reckon that's not quite it. I reckon it takes him back to when he was a much smaller Hurley, chalking his little blackboard and thinking how great it would be to do this when he was older, in grown-up clothes instead of a romper suit. Also, chalk is good to flick at people to wake them up in class.

I was still working on my pic when Dad came home, and I carried on until Mum yelled up that there was food on the table getting COLD. I went down to keep her quiet and fill my chops, but came back immediately afterwards to do some more to my drawing. I'd snaffled one of Mum's dusters earlier to rub out little bits that had gone wrong or that I wanted to improve, and the picture was pretty good by the time Angie rang me on my mobile.

'Are you coming over here or are we coming over there?' she said, without so much as a 'Hi Jig, it's me, Ange, how ya doing?'

'Why does anyone have to go anywhere?' I asked.

'Because things have to be discussed.'

'What things?'

'Five minutes,' she snapped. 'Here! And don't be late!'

That's the trouble with friends. Expect you to be there when they say and talk about things you don't necessarily want to. I stayed put, working on my drawing.

'Jiggy McCue!'

Angie again. This time on the landline in the hall because my mother made me go down when she heard who it was.

'What!'

'Your phone's off.'

'I know.'

'Why?'

'Because I don't want to talk to anyone.'

'Including me?'

'Yes.'

'Why, what have I done?'

'I'm hanging up now,' I said.

'Don't you dare.'

I hung up. Went back upstairs. Got on with the last bit of my drawing. I was pleased with it. Very pleased. And right there in the corner there was still that little picture of the fireman from the telly. I was glad I'd kept the old picture. Me then and me now, past and present. Made me feel kind of warm inside.

When the doorbell went in the distance I didn't think about it. Didn't care who it was. I'd just finished my picture and I liked it so much that I decided to sign it. I signed it like this:

J. Van McCue
The Present Day

I'd just written this when my bedroom door flew open and Pete and Angie walked in.

'What are you doing here?' I said, whirling from the board like I'd been caught drawing something rude.

'Your dad said to come up,' Angie said.

'Without even *asking*?'

'He did ask. He said, "Would you like to go up?" we said, "Sure," and here we are.'

'What do you want?'

'First off, Pete has something to show you.'

Pete was wearing the multi-coloured woolly bobble hat again, right down over his ears. He gripped the bobble and tugged it upward, slowly, dramatically. As you'd expect, with every centimetre more bare head was revealed. What you wouldn't expect was that it wasn't as bare as it had been last time I saw it. The single word I'd written in the Concrete Garden was still in place but it wasn't easy to find it now because his entire upper skull, starting just above the eyebrows, was absolutely covered in graffiti.

'It was you, wasn't it,' Pete said, narrowing his eyes at me.

'Me?' I replied, shocked. 'Pete, have you seen the *spelling*?'

'How could I? It's back to front in mirrors.'

'He wouldn't notice anyway,' Angie muttered.

I walked round him, scanning his head from all angles.

'Some of this could get you arrested,' I said. 'Imagine the police mug shots!'

'It isn't funny!' Pete said.

'I'm not laughing.'

Ange and I eyed one another over his topknot. Her look said it all. My look probably repeated it. The older girls we bumped into as we left him at lunchtime. They must have gone into the Concrete Garden and been inspired by my example while he dozed on. *Very* inspired.

'If it wasn't you, who was it?' Pete said.

'Who knows? Could've been anyone, even one of your fellow baldies celebrating all the new artwork space. When did you notice it?'

'After I woke up, heard the silence, knew I was the only one not in lessons. I went to the Boys to work out what to say when I joined you lot in History. *That's* when I noticed it.'

'Must have been quite a shock.'

'Shock? I nearly died. Why did you leave me? Why didn't you wake me?'

'You were sleeping so soundly. Thought you'd hear the bell.'

'Well you were wrong.'

'He came home instead of going to class,' Angie said.

'Spent half the afternoon trying to scrub it off,'

said Pete. 'Nothing even makes it *fade*.'

'The hair'll grow back before too long,' I said helpfully.

'Not soon enough. And it won't cover all of this even then.'

'You could always go to Zappa's Jokes for a wig.'

'A wig?'

'Great selection. Said so yourself last time we were there.'

'I thought so too when I was looking for the thing to get Julia Frame with,' Angie said. 'I loved the vampire.'

'Vampire?' said Pete.

'Vampire wig. Not for you, though. Need something like the seventies rocker to cover that head.'

'Or the green clown wig,' I suggested.

'People might expect him to juggle in the green clown wig.'

'How about the Afro?'

She shook her head. 'The Afro isn't Pete. The hippy now. Come half way down his back, the hippy would. They throw in a pair of flower-shaped glasses with the hippy.'

161

'I liked the dreadlocks,' I said.

'Mm, maybe. But the King Charles might suit him better.'

'Nah, he'd look like a long-haired poodle in the King Charles.'

Angie grinned. 'There's always the comb-over.'

'I didn't see a comb-over.'

'It was next to the bald one. Not sure who'd want a bald wig, but there are some funny people about.'

'What do you say we change the subject?' Pete said, yanking his hat back on.

'We haven't gone through all the wigs yet,' I said.

'Don't bother. The subject. Change it.'

We thought for a minute. Subject, subject. Funny how there's always a subject shortage when someone tells you to change to another.

'Tell us why you ran out of Mr Hurley's class bent double,' Angie said eventually.

'Not that subject,' I said.

'Yes, that subject. I want to know.'

'Well I don't want to talk about it.'

She gripped me by the shoulders and hung her nose on mine, which wasn't as threatening as she thought because it made her all blurry.

'Talk, McCue, or you're a lamb cutlet.'

'Ange...'

'What?'

'Have you been eating garlic?'

She pulled back like I'd jabbed her nose with a pin.

'I *knew* there was garlic in that chicken at tea! Mum said there wasn't, but I knew there was. Who's got some gum?'

I took an almost new pack out of my pocket. 'Cost you,' I said.

She snatched the pack and crammed three pieces into her trap. I snatched back what was left.

'I had the chicken too,' Pete said, holding out a hand.

I stuffed the slim pack back in my pocket. 'Lucky you.'

'You're the one that's lucky,' said Ange, chewing madly.

'Me, lucky? Since when have I been lucky?'

'Since today's detention was cancelled. If it hadn't been and you hadn't turned up you'd have been right in it on Monday.'

'Why was it cancelled?'

'The word is that Mr Lubelski finally heard about it and told Dakin it wasn't our fault we were late for his class. Why did you skedaddle from History?'

'I was sick.'

'Sick?'

'Of History.'

'Well, Hurley's not very happy about that.'

'Hurley's never happy. And guess what. I don't care. I won't have to put up with this for very much longer. On Tuesday I turn thirteen. Be a whole year closer to the big day I walk out the school gates forever, a free man.'

'Traitor,' Pete said.

'Traitor? Why?'

'Won't be one of us any more when you're thirteen.'

'You'll be thirteen not long after. What'll that make you?'

'A teenager.' He eyed the little blackboard and easel on my desk. 'Isn't that a bit young for you even *before* your birthday?'

'I was just doodling.' No point telling him he was

looking at a work of genius. Pete's about as big on art as I am on football.

'Are you going to tell us why you ran out of class all bent over like bombs were falling and didn't come back?' Angie asked.

'Well–' I said reluctantly.

'Come on, Jig.'

'When I ran out, did the room look any different?'

'Different how?'

'Like the walls had come in and the ceiling was lower.'

'Not that I noticed.'

'All right, I'll tell you. But the first person to say they don't believe me goes down the stairs head first.'

So I told them. Told them everything. About Hurley's classroom closing in and the corridor turning into a tunnel, about a spooky Ryan appearing in my room at night, about going into the girls' toilets–

'You went in the girls' *toilets*?' Pete gasped.

–about the red desert with the white sun, and the pip-pip-pip screen that went piiiiiiiiiiiiiiiiiiiiiiiiiiiiiiiiiiiiiiiiiiiiiiii when the little blips flattened into three straight lines. I told them about my frantic scoot to the hospital to see if Ryan had died, and about meeting Mrs Ryan there, and finding Ryan alive and smiling like he'd done something clever. I also told them about the revolving doors, and Ryan's voice in my head saying, 'This vengeance deal is a blast, now what shall we do next?'.

It was when I told them this bit, the last bit, that Pete said, 'What a load of cobblers,' and I thumped him.

Chapter Sixteen

A while back, Pete came up with this theory that none of us are real. That's you, me, him, everyone, along with the world we live in. According to Pete our homes, teachers, shops, street lamps, trees, you name it, are all out of someone's imagination. We're in a computer simulation put together by this giant kid in his bedroom. The giant kid chose the colour of our eyes, the shape of our noses, our hairstyles, the works.

'Someone *made* Eejit Atkins?' I said when I heard this.

'It's called Unintelligent Design,' said Angie.

'The big kid constructed us on his PC,' Pete said. 'He gave us our names, our families and friends, built our town, our lousy school, then he put all these obstacles in our way and sat back to laugh at the way we dealt with them.'

'Or failed to deal with them?' I said.

'Yeah. Or failed to. The swine.'

It would have been easy to tell him he was talking like a frog's behind, but Pete doesn't get too many off-the-wall ideas and it seemed unkind to trash the first one to turn up in months. Besides, he might have been on to something. I mean, don't you ever wonder if the world you're in is as real as it seems? I do. Quite often actually. Sometimes I feel like I'm a character in a novel. Whole series of novels with colourful covers, and the words 'A Jiggy McCue Story' at the top. How wild is *that*!

What I'm saying is, I didn't snigger at Pete's big idea the way he scoffed at my telling of recent events. But in the end, even he got his personalised head round the idea of Ryan messing with me from his hospital bed. Then we started talking seriously about it.

'It's not Ryan who's doing all this, though, is it?' Angie said.

'Of course it's Ryan,' I said. 'Who else would it be?'

'No, I mean it's his brain.'

'His brain? Yes. Obviously. I didn't think it was one of his toes.'

'I mean his body's shut down but his mind's still

active. It's like at night. You're in bed, you're getting some shut-eye, but your brain doesn't switch off. It creates dreams to while away the time till your bod wakes up and gives it more to do.'

'Not only dreams,' I said. 'Nightmares too.'

'Right. And they're totally believable while you're asleep. So maybe it's the same for Ryan now. His body's off the boil, but his brain's still simmering, and it's thinking, "McCue put me here, I'm gonna get him for this, gonna make him suffer," and when he grabbed your hand at the hospital he made a physical connection with you, and because he made that connection he can make you see and hear things.'

'Like the classroom and corridor closing in? The red desert in the girls' toilets? The pip-pip-pip screen?'

'Yes, all that. Ryan's brain put those things in *your* brain and you had no choice but to live through them.'

'Interesting...' said Pete.

'Not when it's your head that's being messed with,' I said.

'I mean the spelling.'

Before I could ask what he meant there was a screech from downstairs. My name. My mother calling it.

'Is there *no* peace?' I said. I went out to the landing. Glowered down. 'I'm busy!'

'You should be,' Mum said from the bottom of the stairs. 'You have homework.'

'Mother, haven't you heard? It's Friday. School's out for the week. I don't celebrate the start of the weekend with homework.'

'Jiggy, you're behind with it. You must catch up if you want to stay out of detention.'

'Stay out of detention?' I said. 'I wouldn't know how. If I don't get one for not handing in my homework on time I get one for not doing it right, and if I don't get one for that I get one for something else. It's the system. They get you whatever you do.'

'Speaking of which,' she said, 'weren't you supposed to be in detention after school today?'

'No, it was scrapped. Teacher was having a new face fitted. Now do you mind, we're talking here.'

I returned to my room. And saw something that turned my saliva to sawdust. Pete was writing with a piece of chalk on my little kiddie blackboard – which he'd just wiped clean with my mother's duster. My brilliant signed drawing of the pirate ship and the sea battle were gone. So was the little bit of fireman from my youth.

'He did it before I could stop him,' Angie said as I sank tragically onto the bed. 'But you did say it was only a doodle–'

'Yeh. So I did.'

Pete turned to show us what he'd written on the board.

RYANS BRAYN

'See? Ryan and Brayn, same letters apart from the 'B'. Same letters, different order. Even better if we call him by his first name.'

He put a 'B' in front of Ryan to show us. Now it read:

BRYANS BRAYN

'That's not how you spell "brain",' Angie said.

'Course it is, how else would you spell it?'

She grabbed the duster, carefully rubbed out the second 'Y', and filled the gap with an 'I'. Now it looked like this:

BRYANS BRAIN

'You sure about that?' Pete said.

'Absolutely,' said Angie.

'I prefer it the other way.'

'You might prefer it, but it's wrong. This'd look better if Ryan's first name was spelt with an "i" like most other Brians, but it isn't.'

'Uh?' Pete said. He was on a serious learning curve here.

Angie rubbed out the first 'Y' and again put in an 'I', so it read:

BRIANS BRAIN

I groaned. I was still deep in my trauma about what Pete had done to my drawings, but what they were missing out of the words they were fooling with was making my palms sweat.

'What's with you?' Angie asked me.

172

I aimed a shaky finger at the board. She misunderstood.

'I told you, he did it before I could stop him.'

I didn't mean that, and would have said so, but Pete got in first. 'If the "S" wasn't there we'd have all the same letters,' he said. 'Like with Bryan and Brayn.'

He dabbed the board with the duster. Now it read:

BRIAN   BRAIN

Angie clucked like an old hen. 'Garrett, that makes *no* sense.'

'Why does it have to make sense?' Pete said.

'Because I say so.'

She put the 'S' back. Then she put the 'Y' in place of the first 'I' again, and we were back to:

BRYANS   BRAIN

'Lose the first "B",' I said, making a superhuman effort to get over the loss of my beautiful new picture and my childhood.

173

'What?' said Ange.

'Lose the first "B".'

She hesitated. 'I really think that while he's in hospital we ought to—'

'Lose it. This is my room and I want it gone. Now!'

She frowned at me. There aren't many people of my height who can get away with talking to her like that, and I wasn't one of them. But she must have noticed that I wasn't my usual cheery self because she rubbed the 'B' out, which put it back to:

RYANS BRAIN

'And while you're at it...' I said.

'While I'm at it what?'

I nodded at the blackboard. 'Ange, I'm hyperventilating here.'

She stood back from the board, checked it over, saw what I meant. 'Yeah. Right. Knew there was something.'

She rubbed out 'RYANS' and rewrote it to make room for the little thing that was bugging me by not being there. Now it read:

RYAN'S BRAIN

'Thanks,' I said, breathing more easily.

I'd better tell you about this or you'll think I'm weird. My mother started teaching me to read while I was still in nappies. Good for her, you might say, but because she has to have everything absolutely right, she didn't just teach me to read, she made sure I knew where all the punctuation marks went from my first ten-word picture book, through Postman Pat and beyond. To get me to remember, she made me say their names when I started to read out loud. And it became a habit. Took me years to stop saying the punctuation when we had to stand up to read in class. Example:

The second customer was different semi-colon, as bad-hyphen-tempered as the first was jolly, full-stop. Open quotes, capital I, apostrophe double L, buy that puppet, comma, close quotes, said the bad-hyphen-tempered man, full-stop. Open quotes, capital I, have a job for him, comma, and, capital I, think he-apostrophe-double L

175

make my fortune, full-stop, close quotes.

I still get twitchy about punctuation. I can be a bit sloppy when I scribble all this personal stuff, but I'm the only kid I know who can't send a text message without apostrophes and caps. Sometimes I rebel and miss them out deliberately, but I feel bad for hours. I even break into a jig occasionally. A jig of guilt. That mother of mine has a lot to answer for.

Angie feels a bit like me about punctuation, but she isn't a fanatic. Pete, though. Pete's the opposite.

'I hate those things!' he cried, grabbing the duster and rubbing the friendly little mark off the board. Now we had:

RYAN S BRAIN

I jumped up. 'Hold him, Ange!'

She pinned his arms behind him while I put the apostrophe back. 'Take it out again,' she said to Pete, 'and I take *you* out.'

'Now that we know what we're talking about,' I said then, 'we might as well go to the next level, starting with…'

Under the words RYAN'S BRAIN I drew this picture:

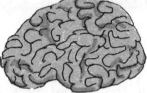

P & A sat on the end of the bed while I was doing this. I was vaguely aware of Pete fiddling with the phone I'd tossed there, but I was too involved in my drawing to bother about it. I drew some bubbles around the brain, and lines from the brain to them, then I picked up my Kings and Queens of Sweden ruler and tapped the board with it.

'This is Ryan's Brain,' I said. 'These lines join the brain to these bubbles. Now what do you think should go in the bubbles?'

'Don't get you,' Angie said.

'I want to fill the bubbles with ideas of the sort of things a brain like Ryan's would come up with to get back at me, so I can be ready for them. Ideas please.'

They looked at one another the way kids do in lessons when Mr Hurley or one of the other teachy types asks for contributions.

'Come on!' I said sternly from the front of the class. 'I want input, input.' I rapped the board again. 'What is Ryan's brain likely to dream up next?'

'How would we know?' Pete said.

I frowned at the stupid boy. 'Well, of course you don't *know*. I don't *know*. But that doesn't mean you can't imagine the *sort* of thing Ryan would think of.'

He shrugged. 'He's your worst enemy, not ours. You should know the way his mind works better than us.' He punched some numbers on my phone.

'Hey,' I said. 'I have to pay for that.'

'So send me the bill.'

'Who're you ringing?'

He put the thing to his ear. 'Dunno.'

'Then what—?'

'Wait.'

We waited. After a few rings, someone at the other end picked up.

'Hello?' Pete said. 'Is Mr Wall there?' Pause. 'Well, is Mrs Wall there?' Pause. 'There are no Walls there?' Pause. 'So how does your roof stay up?'

178

He clicked off and fell back on the bed, kicking his stupid legs in the air. When he'd got over it I asked him to leave. Angie too. I had work to do. Homework. A backlog.

Chapter Seventeen

Saturday morning. No visits from Ryan in the night, so I didn't feel too bad as I went downstairs. My mother was at the front door in her dressing gown, hair in a towel because she'd just washed it (the hair), leaning out, peering around the step. I asked what was up. She showed me a card the postman had shoved through the letterbox. It was one of those post office cards with little boxes on, and words to go with them.

☐ Your post person called today and obtained no reply. Please phone the depot (see number at bottom) to arrange for another delivery attempt.

☐ Your post person has left a package or parcel with your neighbour at number...

☑ Your post person has left a package or parcel in a secure location.

The third box had a tick in it. 'That man,' Mum said. 'He claims that he rings the bell, but I've never *yet* heard it when he has something too big for the flap. Usually he leaves it on the step.'

'It's Stallone,' I said.

'Stallone?'

'Postie's afraid that if someone opens the door the mad mog'll shoot out and sink some of those fangs in his leg.'

'Stallone wouldn't do that.'

'Oh no? His fur goes up whenever he sees the bloke. I think it's the uniform. Brushed up against too many yapping dogs on its rounds, and Stallone can smell 'em – can't you, Stall?'

Stallone looked up from the slipper he was trying to tear apart with his teeth. Mum pulled the slipper out of his mouth, mainly because her foot was still in it.

'I don't even know what it is,' she said.

'What what is?'

'The package or parcel that's now in a secure location. As for *where*... Do me a favour, pop out and look, will you?'

'I'm not dressed,' I said.

'Well neither am I.'

'So wait till you are.'

She sucked her shoulders in, muttered something about the members of her family being *so* unhelpful, and stalked into the kitchen. I followed her, walking not stalking, because the kitchen's where the grub is. The adjoining door to the garage was open. Mum leaned through it.

'Mel...'

I heard a grunty reply and went to look over her shoulder. My father was on his knees on the floor of the garage trying to break into the heavy-duty cardboard box that been left with Mrs O next door yesterday while everyone in our house was out. The words *Made in Beijing* were printed on the sides of the box, so we had a fair idea what was in it. A few months ago Dad had entered this competition. I don't know what the entrants had to do, but first prize was an all-expenses-paid trip for two to China. Second prize was a Chinese bike for one. Dad had won the second prize, and here it was. Ever since he heard he'd won a bike, he'd been all dreamy about what was going to happen when it arrived. The picture he painted was of him going on long rides with cheese-and-chutney sandwiches and a happy grin every time he heaved himself out of his armchair. There was just one snag, but he hadn't realised it yet. The snag was that my dad has a problem getting even the simplest things open. He can't get into a new packet of tea or a CD or DVD or anything else without a fight. He's always yelling 'PACKAGING!' and throwing unopened things in corners. The *Made in Beijing* box, which had huge iron staples along every join, looked too big and heavy to throw into corners, so I was quite interested to see how he got on with it.

'Mel, have you ordered anything?' Mum asked him.

'Yeah. I ordered a beer and it didn't come.'

'Glad to hear it at nine-thirty a.m.'

'Nine-twenty-six,' I said. I like to be right about these things. 'And fifteen seconds. Sixteen, seventeen, eighteen...'

'You haven't sent me anything, have you?' Mum said.

'Who, me?' I said.

'Your father.'

Dad looked up with a frown. 'Sent you anything?'

'For our...you know.'

'No, should I have done?'

'Well, it might have been nice, but...' She sighed. 'Not expecting anything yourself in the post, are you?'

'No.'

'Only the postman's been, and he's left something, and I don't know what it is.'

'So open it and find out.'

'I would if I knew where it was. He's hidden it in the front garden.'

'In a secure location,' I said over her shoulder.

'Well go and look for it. Or don't look for it. Up to you, I don't care, problems of my own here.'

Mum returned to the hall, but I stayed, watching my father struggling with the box. 'Need a hand?' I asked after a while.

He glanced up at me, almost said, 'Wouldn't mind,' but must have caught the glint in my eye, and didn't. He knew that glint. Knew what it meant. We have this understanding, Dad and I. If he wants my help with something he knows there's a price. I don't mean he has to shell out money. Not always. Sometimes he pays me back with a tiny fib

184

to get me out of doing something for Mum, or to cover me for something she thinks I should have done, or to take my side when I want something she'd be totally against. He knows that I don't forget when he owes me either. I keep a little book with everything listed in columns, showing what I did for him and what's due to me in return.

'I can do it,' he growled. 'It's only a sodding box, after all.'

'Yeah, the big challenge lies ahead,' I said.

'Big challenge?'

'Putting together what's inside.'

'Piece of cake. It's a bike. A prize bike. They wouldn't send a prize in kit form.'

'That box is not full bike size,' I pointed out.

He ran his eyes over it. 'There'll be a couple of the larger bits to put together, that's all. Nothing complicated.'

'I've heard that before,' I said, going back to the kitchen.

I loaded some Super Choco Bombs into a bowl, drowned them with milk, and sat down to feed my face. There was a card on the table, a greetings card sort of card, standing up beside an envelope someone had torn open. The envelope had the word 'Mel' on it and on the front of the card there was a painting of two people sitting by a river holding hands. I looked inside. A sloppy rhyme about eternal love that didn't sound like something either of my parents would say. My mother had written her name under this twaddle, with a row of little crosses like something from a cemetery. It was an anniversary card. Today was my parents' wedding anniversary, the brass one or something. I'd forgotten all about it.

'Happy anniversary, Mum!' I bawled to my mother, who was still trying to work out where the secure location might be from the front door.

'Thank you, Jiggy,' she answered with a voice like a tray of ice cubes. 'Good to know *someone* remembered.'

I ate some more cereal. I felt pretty good actually. Nothing bad had happened since yesterday afternoon, I'd had an uninterrupted night's sleep and a little lie-in, and today looked like being a typical what-can-I-do-I'm-so-bored Saturday. With any luck, I thought, Ryan's brain has run out of steam, or whatever it is brains run out of. I was still thinking this, cheerfully chucking Super Choco Bombs past my tonsils, when something blocked out the light at the windows. I looked up, and...

You know how it is when you're on one side of a window and someone puts their open mouth against the other side and their lips spread out and go all flat? Well, this is what I was looking at. A mouth on the window, wide open, lips squashed against it. Might have made me jump if I'd looked up and it was Pete or someone. But it wasn't Pete or someone. I couldn't tell who it was because all I could see was mouth. Why could I only see mouth? Because it *covered* the window. I mean the *whole* window. The window that went almost from one end of the kitchen to the other.

I put my spoon down. Slowly. I stood up. Slowly. I pushed my chair back. Slowly. Then I opened my own mouth, not because I wanted to copy the giant one that was covering the window, but because it had something to say.

'MUUUUUUUUUUUUUUUUM.'

There was a pause, then the parent being summoned looked in. 'What are you shouting for?'

I pointed at the window.

'What?' she said, looking.

'The mouth.'

She went tense. 'Mouse? Where?'

'Not mouse. *Mouth.*'

'Mouth?'

I shut my eyes in frustration. Was she blind?

I opened them again. There were houses and a bit of sky where the mouth had been.

'It's gone,' I said.

'What's gone?'

'The giant mouth that covered the window. Ryan's mouth.'

'Ryan's mouth? Jiggy, what are you—'

'Had to be his. But huger than usual. A lot huger. It was horrible. He needs to see a dentist when he gets out of hospital.'

I got up and went to the window. No giant mouths loitered in the front garden. The only life out there was Stallone doing his business on a patch of earth by the fence.

I turned back to the table. Mum was skidding her eyes through the ocean of small print on the side of the packet of Super Choco Bombs. 'It must be one of these,' she said. 'But which one? There

188

are so many and they add new ones all the time. Jiggy, you're not eating any more of these.'

She took the packet to the flip-top bin behind the door and rammed it in. Then she went back to the table for my bowl, and flushed the last of my favourite cereal down the waste disposal. Well, I'd lost my appetite anyway.

I went upstairs, holding the rail all the way because my legs were a bit shaky after the mouth incident. Suddenly there were just two things I was sure about. The first was that I'd been wrong thinking that Ryan was done with me. The second thing was that I didn't want to be alone when the next thing happened.

Up in my room, I grabbed my phone and jabbed a button.

'Ange, I have to see you.'

'Well you'll have to wait. Conditioner's running down my back.'

'Conditioner?'

'I'm washing my hair.'

'You too? Is hair washing some Saturday morning ritual that all female types are programmed to do or something?'

'I don't do it every Saturday morning,' she snapped, 'but I am *this* Saturday morning, all right? Wish I'd known I had to check with you first because you were absolutely the *last* person I thought to ask.'

'Look, this is urgent,' I said. 'A "One for all" situation.'

'Oh, it would be, wouldn't it, when it couldn't be *less* convenient! Well, come over if you must.'

'No. I don't want to be indoors. Need to be out in the open. Somewhere like the park.'

'Why have you got to be outside?'

'Because I'll feel safer in wide open spaces.'

'Jig, has something happened?'

'Of course something's happened. You don't think I'd disturb your holy hairwash for nothing, do you? Tell you about it when I see you. Five minutes.'

'Half an hour. I have to rinse my hair.'

'That'll take thirty seconds.'

'And dry it.'

'I leave mine to dry naturally.'

'That's because you don't care how yours looks,' she said.

190

'Nor did you, once upon a time.'

'Once upon a time I was little. You want Pete too?'

'No, but I might need to put him between me and whatever.'

'He might not come. Said last night he's not going out again till his hair grows long enough to cover the graffiti.'

'Twist his arm.'

I rang off.

Chapter Eighteen

I kept looking over my shoulder in the mirror the whole ten seconds it took to clean my teeth, and the whole whatever it took me to get dressed. Mum likes me to make my bed at the weekend, even though she does it tons better than I do, but I didn't want to be alone any longer than I had to, so I left it, went downstairs to the tune of the hair dryer from my parents' room. Because I didn't want to be alone and had time to kill, I went to the garage to see how Dad was getting on. He'd managed to get the box open with the help of a pair of scissors and a huge screwdriver, but one of his hands was bleeding.

'These staples are lethal!' he said when he saw me.

A truckload of parts lay scattered across the floor – wheels, brakes, gears, pedals, tubes, reflectors, packets of screws and brackets and things, and a bell so big it could have dropped out of Notre Dame and crushed a tourist. There was also a pair of dazzling orange-and-silver stickers that screamed the words LIGHTNING FLASHER.

It was on the tip of my tongue to remind my father that I'd warned him he'd have his work cut out, but I kept it to myself. He stared mournfully at all the bits.

'You need a bloody engineering degree for this lot.'

'Aren't there any instructions?' I asked.

'Oh, there are *instructions* all right.' He waved a long scroll of paper from the box. 'In Tangerine!'

'You mean Mandarine?'

'Yeah, Mandarin. One of the thousand or so languages I don't speak.'

I took the scroll from him. 'The diagrams might help,' I said.

'I'm not so great with diagrams.'

This was true. My father has diagram blindness. And sign blindness. He'll stare at simple shapes for ages trying to work out what they are. It's pretty scary in the car when he's driving somewhere new. 'What's *that* meant to mean?' he shouts as we pass a sign showing a man ramming an umbrella into the ground, and, 'What was the wavy line with the cross above it all about?' as we go over a cliff.

'I'd start with the frame and work outwards,' I said.

'The frame?'

'Those long bits. They probably slot into one another.'

He picked up two of the long bits, one in each hand, looked at them like he was going to bang them together for musical accompaniment, and tried to force the end of one into the wrong end of the other.

'Here,' I said, reaching for them.

He pulled away. 'I can do it! I won't have my own son showing me how to put a lousy bike together!'

'OK.'

'Jiggy!' My mother.

I went through the kitchen to the hall. Looked up the stairs.

'You haven't made your bed.'

'It's airing.'

'It *has* aired. Now come up and *make* it!'

'Oh, Mum!'

'Don't "Oh, Mum" me! Get up here now, you know the rule!'

194

I hunched upstairs. Rules, rules, my life's a jungle of rules. A maze of them. You hear people moan about having a dog's life. They're barking. Dogs have it made compared to kids.

I did my bed in double quick time. A duvet helps. You grab a corner and flip it up, then fall across it and straighten the other corner. Still a chore if you don't want to do it, though. My mother came in just as I finished.

'What do you call that?'

'You mean my bed? I call it a bed, what do you call it?'

'That's not the way to make a bed and you know it.'

She took hold of the duvet at the top end and pulled the whole thing back to the bottom.

'Do it again.'

'Mum!'

'Properly this time. I'll stand here till you do.'

I tugged a corner of the duvet up, then went round and straightened the other corner.

'All right?' I said, standing beside my work.

'No, Jiggy, it's not all right. It's nothing like all right. I've shown you a hundred times how to make a bed.'

'I forget.'

She tut-tutted and pulled the duvet down. 'The first thing you do is fluff up the pillows.' She fluffed up the pillows. Good, I thought, now they'll be lovely and soft tonight. 'Then you smooth out the undersheet.' She smoothed the undersheet with the flat of her hand on one side, then went round the other side to smooth it there too. 'Making *sure*,' she said, glaring at me, 'to brush away all the biscuit crumbs for sweeping up later.' She brushed the biscuit crumbs onto the floor. 'When the sheet is clear and wrinkle-free, you pull the duvet up.' She pulled the duvet up on that side, then went round and pulled the first side up as well. 'Next you go to the foot of the bed...' she went to the foot of the bed, '...take hold of the duvet in both hands...' she took hold of the duvet in both hands '...and give it a good shake to allow the interior to redistribute itself evenly.' Now it was all bulgy and ultra-soft, just the way I like it. 'Finally,' she said, 'you go back to the head of the bed and straighten it there.' She returned to the head of the bed, straightened the duvet on one side, then went round and straightened the other. It looked

196

perfect. It *was* perfect. So comfortable that I couldn't wait to get to bed tonight. 'Now for the hundred and first time have you *got* all that?' she asked.

'Think so.'

'Good. Now let's see you do it.'

She whipped the duvet back, threw herself on the bed to rumple it, and scrunched the pillows so they were like they were when I got up. The only thing she didn't do was scatter biscuit crumbs on the sheet.

After making my bed three times before my bullying mother was satisfied, I went into the front garden to help her look for the secure location the postman had left the mysterious package in. She was wearing a T-shirt she'd bought a couple of days ago from one of the peculiar shops she goes to. Her chest read '99% Fat Free' when she faced you, but if she turned a bit to the left the word 'Free' disappeared. She probably didn't realise this. Maybe I'd tell her sometime. Not now though. Punishment for all the bed-making.

There are about zero places you could call secure in our front garden, but we looked in the two bits of bush, the bit of hedge, under the bits of wall, and behind the four plant pots. Dad slouched out while we were poking about. I asked how the bike was coming.

'Nothing fits,' he said.

'It probably does. You just need to—'

'Nothing *fits*, I tell you!'

'Bet I could do it,' I muttered.

He heard. 'Oh, sure you could. Kids today, you think you know everything. When I was your age I knew nothing.'

'And he's proud of it,' Mum said, lifting one of the plant pots because she obviously thought a package that couldn't go through a letterbox would fit under a plant pot.

'A kid should be a kid,' Dad said.

'I am a kid,' I said.

'Not a pint-sized adult.'

'I'm not a pint-sized adult.'

'Ignorant of the ways of the world and how to do stuff.'

'You mean like putting Chinese bikes together?'

He scowled. 'When I was a kid there was no such thing as Chinese bikes.'

198

'Not even in China?' I asked.

'We'd never heard of China.'

'Bet you wish you hadn't now either.'

'Pretty close to it,' he agreed.

'Mel,' Mum said, 'you've got your boots on.'

She'd wandered over to the fence that separates us from the Atkins's next door. A spade stood in the ground where Dad had left it after a back-breaking two minute gardening marathon last Sunday.

'So?' Dad said, looking at his boots.*

Mum jerked her head. He went to the fence. So did I.

'Looks freshly turned,' Mum said, pointing to a patch of dark earth beside the spade. 'Must be the postman.'

'You think under the ground is a secure location?' I asked.

'He must have been stuck for somewhere else.'

'No,' I said. 'Wherever he put it, it wasn't here.'

'It has to be. It's the only place left.'

'You're wrong.'

She frowned at me. 'Jiggy, if you can't be constructive go and do something else, will you?'

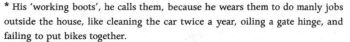

* His 'working boots', he calls them, because he wears them to do manly jobs outside the house, like cleaning the car twice a year, oiling a gate hinge, and failing to put bikes together.

'Suit yourself.'

I strolled over to the weedy little cherry tree she got from the garden centre last autumn. I wasn't going to miss this.

'Dig down,' Mum said to Dad.

'Me?' he said.

'I'd do it myself, but you're the one in boots. It won't take a minute, be just under the surface.'

He snatched the spade and drove it into the patch of dark earth, muttering, 'I should have stayed in the garage.'

While I watched from beside the cherry tree – smiling secretly because only I knew what they were actually digging down to – my eye drifted to the bit above the tree's skinny trunk, where the twiggy branches flopped outward. There, nestled neatly, was a small box shape in brown paper, just too big to get through our letter flap. We hadn't been looking for anything that small, so we hadn't even given the tree a glance.

As I took the little box down I heard Dad say, 'Well, it's a package all right, but I doubt that it came with stamps on.'

'Cover it up,' Mum said.

Dad covered it up.

If they'd heard me out I'd have told them that that was where I'd seen Stallone doing his business just after the giant mouth covered the window, but would they listen? Nah, I'm just a kid.

'Try this one,' I said.

They turned, all set to be annoyed with me as usual. The little box sat on my palm for all to see.

'What's that?'

'Looks like a box,' I said.

'Where did you find it?'

'In this sad excuse for a tree.'

They came over. The box was addressed to Mum, so she took it, without a word of thanks or praise, tore off the wrapping right there and then because she couldn't wait to see what was inside. What she found was a free pair of support tights from a firm who made things for really Golden Oldies. Without a word she marched into the house with the free support tights and the little box. I knew what she was going to do with them. Drop them in the flip-top bin on top of the packet of Super Choco Bombs that she thought had been making me hallucinate.

'Jig!'

Angie, calling from across the road as she and Pete came out of their house.

'Luck with the bike!' I said to my father.

I opened the front gate, patted the BEWARE OF THE CAT sign, and joined the other two Musketeers on the pavement.

Chapter Nineteen

Pete had a different hat on today. The fishing hat his dad wears for not going fishing with my dad, who also has one for not going fishing with him. He (that's Pete) said the other one (that's the multi-coloured woolly bobble hat) made his head itch.

'You persuaded him then,' I said to Angie.

'She threatened to paint my head in my sleep,' said Pete.

'Not a bad idea,' I said. 'Would have covered the words up.'

'She threatened to paint it yellow. I hate yellow.'

'Tell us the latest,' Angie said to me on the way to the park.

I told them about the mouth at the window.

'Maybe it was a reflection,' Pete said.

'Reflection?'

'Of your mouth.'

'Pete, the mouth at the window was the size of a bungalow.'

'Like I said, maybe it was a reflection.'

'So you think Ryan's still on your case,' Angie said.

'I know he is.'

'What are you going to do about it?'

'Short of sneaking into the hospital and pulling the plug on his life-support, I haven't the faintest.'

'Sounds like you're between a rock and a fireplace,' said Pete.

'Hard place,' said Angie.

'What?'

'Rock and a hard place.'

'What are you talking about?'

'You should have said he's between a rock and a hard place.'

'Why would I say that?'

'Because that's the way it goes.'

'Way what goes?'

'The saying. Between a rock and a hard place.'

'I don't get you.'

'I mean he isn't between a rock and a fireplace, he's between a rock and a hard place.'

'Is he?'

'You tell me, you're the one who said it.'

'Me?' said Pete. 'I don't even know what it means.'

We passed the last few shops before the park – the travel agent's, the baker's, the shoe shop with the special offer in the window ('Buy one, get one free') – and strolled through the gates.

Apart from the café that's never open, there's nothing much in the Councillor Snit Memorial Park, just trees, grass, a lake, some benches, but that was fine, I felt less threatened in the middle of so little. There was only one other person there too, a man, some way away, though I wished he was in another park because he'd just let a couple of big brown dogs off the leash and they were running far and wide.

'You know why dogs have wet noses?' Pete asked.

'They have wet noses when they're healthy, not such wet noses when they're less healthy,' Angie said. 'Common knowledge.'

He shook his head. 'They have wet noses because they're always licking them. They do that a lot when they're healthy. When they're not feeling so great they don't lick them so often, so they dry out. I looked it up the other day.'

'What for?'

'Game I was playing on my PC had a dog in it, and its nose was all wet and slobbery, and I got to wondering about it. I also found out that dogs' noses run quite a lot. Ask me why.'

Angie sighed. 'Why do dogs' noses run a lot, Pete?'

'They need the exercise.'

'Hey, look at those horses,' I said.

'Horses?' said Angie.

I couldn't see where they'd come from so suddenly, but there were a couple of dozen of them, all spread out and trotting our way.

'Doesn't seem to be anyone with them,' I said. 'No minders, no riders.'

'What's he on about?' Pete said.

'Look, they're picking up speed. They're heading for the gates. We're right in their path.'

You could hear them now. If someone didn't take charge of them soon we'd be hoofed to pulp.

'Come on!' I said.

I was about to start running when Angie gripped my shoulders with both hands and said 'Jig!' like someone whose next words will be, 'Get a hold of yourself, they're only horses.'

But when she gripped me she gave a little jump, and her hands flew away as if they'd been stung. Then she frowned like she'd just heard something for the first time. She turned her head. Looked towards the horses, now galloping our way at speed.

'Where did they…?'

And then she was running, and shouting for us to run too. I was already on my way. I glanced back at Pete. He was still standing there. Didn't seem bothered that the horses were heading straight for him. That any minute they would gallop over him.

'Pete!' I yelled. 'Move it!'

He said something, but the hooves were so loud now that I didn't catch it. Didn't much matter what he said anyway because just then the horses swerved, the whole lot of them. Came after me and Angie.

The next bit is kind of a blur. Ange and I ran like crazy while the hooves got closer and closer. Any second they'd be up with us, on us, over us, and all that would be left of us would be McCue and Mint indentations in the grass.

'That big tree over there!' Angie screamed.

It was our only hope. A slight change of direction and we might just get out of their path in time. We were so terrified that we stopped looking over our shoulders, just ran and ran, heads down, arms flying. A dozen metres to the tree, that was all it was, a dozen metres and—

'Oh no!'

The hooves had changed direction again. Not only that, they'd speeded up even more. They were so close now, so close, almost deafening, but we made it to the tree, made it with split seconds to spare. Behind the trunk, Angie and I clung to one another, gasping for breath, waiting for the horses to gallop by. And they did. The sound of them anyway. But *only* the sound.

The horses had become invisible!

We stared after the coconutty rhythm fading into the distance. Angie was the first to find some words. Three of them.

'What was that?'

I found another one. 'Ryan.'

'Ryan?'

'Ryan's brain, horsing about.'

Pete strolled round the trunk and stood in front of us, blocking our view of the empty park. He had his hands in his pockets and a very Garretty smirk on his face.

'Can anyone join in,' he said, 'or is this a two-twerp game?'

Chapter Twenty

Pete didn't believe a word of it, even from Angie. 'If you were chased by a load of horses I think I'd have noticed,' he said. 'Also...' he wandered away, peering at the ground, '...there'd be hoof prints. And there isn't one. Mind you, if there was only one hoof print it'd be a pretty freaky horse.'

'Like I said last night,' Angie said to me, 'it's all in the mind. Ryan's mind first, then yours. Except this time I experienced it too. I really thought those hooves were going to trash my bones.'

'You didn't at first.'

'No. Not till I grabbed your shoulders.'

'You think the shoulder grabbing made the diff?'

'Must have. When I grabbed you, you passed the connection on to me.'

'Even through clothing?'

'Even through clothing. I'm on the receiving end too now. Thanks a lot, pal.'

Pete came back to us. 'OK, what is it? You two

setting me up for an out-of-season April Fool or something? Chased by invisible horses – per-*lease*.'

'You can believe it or you can stand on your head in a bucket of tripe,' Angie said. 'It happened. Every word Jiggy's told us is true. Well maybe not every word. Maybe not even most words. But the words about what Ryan's been putting him through, they're true.'

Pete still wasn't convinced. He'd seen and heard nothing.

But then he did see something. Something that interested him and no one else. A little mouse, nosing around in the grass like it had lost something. Pete loves mice. Mice and other creatures like them. If he was allowed he would fill his bedroom with guinea pigs, hamsters, gerbils, even rats. Nearest he gets is a couple of posters on his wall. He picked the mouse up. It didn't seem to mind.

'Mice sing,' he said, stroking the little grey head.

'They what?' I said.

'Male mice. Sing to female mice. I read it in a magazine.'

'What sort of thing?'

'What sort of thing?'

'What sort of music?'

'How would I know? I've never heard them.'

'So who has?' Angie wanted to know.

'No one. The human ear *can't* hear them.'

'Who says?'

'Scientists.'

'Don't scientists have human ears then?'

'What do you mean?'

'Well, if scientists have human ears and the singing mice can't be *heard* by human ears, how did the human ears of the scientists know they were singing?'

'The article didn't say. Maybe they use microphones.'

He put the mouse gently back in the grass and we stood watching it snuffle around down there. It was quite cute actually. The big black bird that swooped down must have thought so too, because it closed its beak on the mouse and carried it off into the sky to either keep as a pet or rip its cute little heart out.

'Nature,' I said. 'Gets you right there, doesn't it?'

'Ooh,' Angie said suddenly.

I was about to ask what she was oohing for when I said it too, for the same reason. Something was tickling our legs. We looked down to see what, and saw lots of little grey mice streaming up us like they'd just spotted a big hunk of Farmhouse Cheddar at the top.

Now Ange and I can take or leave mice in ones and twos when they're squeaking quietly in grass, or even tiptoeing across floorboards and carpets like they used to occasionally in our old houses. It's a bit different when there's a bunch of them heading north from your ankles. It's the kind of difference that makes you go prickly-cold all over, and stamp your feet, and run round in small circles shaking your fingers like they have cobwebs on them, which is what we did.

While we were doing this I heard Pete in the background asking what we were up to now.

'Can't you *see*?' I answered.

'See what?'

These mice were invisible to him. He'd seen the one that was now flying EasyBird to the sun, but he couldn't see the batch swarming up us. Which meant that Ryan's brain had sent them.

But the leg mice were nothing compared to what came half a handful of seconds later. Lightning, whole bolts of it, zapping the ground around our feet – just mine and Angie's again – and thunder so loud it almost burst the drums of our ears. We tried covering our ears with one hand while swatting the mice with the other, but that only stopped us being deafened in one ear apiece and meant that some mice got nearer the personals than they would have otherwise.

We were still trying to deal with all this when something else happened. You know how you see shapes and faces in clouds sometimes? Well suddenly there were shapes and faces in the clouds above us. The shapes and faces of cats. Two of them. Huge snarling cats whose mouths got wider and wider and nearer and nearer, not to nibble the mice on our legs, but to snack on me and Ange. Now I've been at the pointy end of Stallone's fangs so many times it's like he has a season ticket to me, but even I was worried by those two. They might only have been made of cloud, but they were coming for me, for us, and when something that big looks that mean and hungry you can't help

214

being a tad nervous, whatever it's made of. If I hadn't already been dancing my legs off to keep the mice down and dodge the lightning I'd have broken into a twitch-and-tap that could have taken me over the horizon.

But before the cats could get us, something else happened. The cloud cats were just over our heads with their huge gaping jaws, the thunder was still roaring, the lightning was still zapping, the mice were still trying to reach our peaks, when something fierce started tugging at the ankle of my jeans. I yanked my leg to try and free it, but the fierce something wouldn't let go. Maybe it was because of this new thing, maybe it wasn't, but the thunder and lightning stopped just like that, the cloud cats dissolved, the mice vanished from our legs, and a voice shouted in the distance.

'Stand still and they'll lose interest!'

The man we'd seen across the park when we came in. The one with the dogs that weren't on leads. The dogs that had run up while we were dodging lightning, trying to cover our ears, swat mice and avoid being gobbled by cats in the clouds. One of the dogs had the ankle of my jeans in its teeth and the other had got hold of Angie's sleeve. We didn't stand still like the man told us to.

'Get off me, get off me, get *OFF* me!' Angie bawled, trying to shake the brute attached to her sleeve, while I shouted something similar but ruder and tried to stamp on the other dog's paws.[1]

The man ran up, shouting at the dogs, but they were more interested in getting past the material in their mouths and sinking their teeth into juicy human flesh. Ange and I pulled and pulled, and the man shouted and shouted, and the dogs ignored him and ignored him, and all this might have gone on till bedtime if Pete hadn't come to the rescue. Yes, Pete Garrett, for once acting like a Musketeer. He ran at the dogs with a bit of branch he'd found and started whacking them. Now the man was yelling at him instead of the dogs, but Pete kept on whacking, shouting things like 'Grrr!', 'Woof off!', 'Go, go, go!' until they let go of Ange and me, and fled, fast as whippets.[2]

The man turned to Pete.

'You hit my dogs,' he said in disbelief.

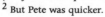

[1] No animals were harmed by Angie or me during the writing of this scene. (They were too quick for us.)
[2] But Pete was quicker.

Pete dropped the branch. 'Someone had to do something.'

'They would have let go in a minute.'

'In a *minute*?' said Angie, looking at her torn sleeve. 'Look what that brute did to my coat!'

'And my jeans!' I said, though my jeans weren't torn.

'It's your own fault for playing the fool,' the man said.

Angie narrowed her eyes. 'Playing the fool? We were trying to swat the mice, dodge the storm, and avoid the cloud cats!'

'You were what?'

'Angie…' I said.

'But whatever we were doing–' she was really angry '–it didn't entitle you to set your wild dogs on us!'

'They're not wild, they're domestic animals, and I didn't–'

'I want your name and address,' she said, marching up to him.

'Eh?'

She stopped in front of him, scowling. God, she looked mean.

'Our parents'll have you for this. They'll have the law on you. They'll have those animals put down.'

'I did tell you not to move,' the man said feebly.

'Not move? This isn't a sculpture park, it's a park for people. People, not dogs! Didn't you see the notice about keeping dogs on leads? What's your name, I'm going to report you.'

'Brutus! Cassius!'

These weren't the man's names. He'd shouted them after the dogs, who were zooming towards the boating lake. When they didn't reply he went after them, bawling their names over and over, like repeating them would make them turn around and come back wagging their doggy tails. Angie yelled something too, about seeing him in court, but he kept going. When it was clear that he also wasn't coming back, she turned to Pete.

'Did something useful for once in your life there.'

'Don't mention it,' he said. He looked quite proud of himself.

'OK, I won't. As for you...' She turned to me. 'Keep your distance. I don't want to see you ever again.'

'What?' I said, shocked.

218

'Or at least till this is all over.'

'But Ange,' I said as she turned away.

'Don't "but Ange" me,' she said, walking.

'Aw, come on. One for all and all for–'

She hung her hands on her ears and stuck her elbows out, singing 'La-la-la-la-la-a-la,' very loudly as she scooted towards the gates.

'Are you going to abandon me too?' I said to Pete as we watched her go.

He turned the brim of his dad's fishing hat up. 'I would if I knew what all the fuss was about.'

'You do know. Ryan's brain chucking its weight about. Not the dogs though. The dogs were real. Something's got to be done about this.'

'The dogs?'

'The brain. Will you come to the hospital with me?'

'It's all right, you don't have to thank me for saving you from being torn to blood-soaked pieces by the dogs.'

'OK. Will you?'

'Will I what?'

'Come to the hospital.'

'What, to see the toe-rag again?'

'The unconscious toe-rag. I have to talk to him. Try and reason with him in his sleep. Get him to chain his brain before things get even worse. Come on, Pete. I need someone there with me, and there's only you left.'

He shrugged. He had nothing better to do. We headed for the gates.

Chapter Twenty-one

The hospital was quite busy, probably because it was Saturday, when a lot of people want to visit a lot of other people in bed. There was a scrum round the front desk again, so we slid by. I had no idea how we were going to get in to see Ryan this time, but as we approached the Intensive Care sign two nurses came out and went in different directions. That didn't mean there weren't any more nurses inside, but instead of ringing the bell I pushed one of the doors back a bit and peeked in to see. We were in luck. No one at the nursy desk.

We crept in.

All three of the beds were occupied today. The fat man was still listening to music or a hypnotist and in the spare bed there was a boy of sixteen, seventeen, with one plastered leg in the air and two plastered arms. He had a pair of huge swollen eyes, which were just about open, staring at the ceiling. Must have been quite a Friday night.

Ryan didn't look much different, except the smile had worn off and the bruise on his forehead looked a bit better. His eyes were still closed. Unfortunately for us, his mum was there again. And she wasn't alone this time. Mr Ryan sat next to her on one side of the bed and a boy of about eight stood on the other. The boy was small and weedy, and he had this weird rust-coloured hair that stood up in spikes like he'd had a big shock.

'Oh, it's Bryan's friend,' Mrs Ryan said before we could back out. 'And another friend too, how nice. Make way, Russ.' The little boy made some space for me and Pete to stand with him on that side. 'I don't think you know my husband, do you?' Mrs R said, touching Mr Ryan's shoulder.

I shook my head for both of us. We'd seen Mr Ryan once before, from a distance, but I don't think he noticed us.* Couldn't miss us this time, though he looked like he'd rather.

'And our other son, Russell.'

Pete and I glanced at one another. We hadn't known Ryan had a little brother. The kid ignored Pete, but he clocked me with these sharp, dark eyes that made me uncomfortable. He didn't look

---

* See *Nudie Dudie*, the day Ryan showed off his birthday suit on his front step.

any friendlier than his old man.

Mrs Ryan was holding Bry-Ry's hand. 'The nurses said he gave a little laugh a while ago,' she said to Pete and me.

'Little laugh?' I said.

'He must have been dreaming something lovely. Or funny. That's nice, isn't it?'

'Yeah, that's terrific.'

'Come on, June,' Mr Ryan said, standing up suddenly.

'Oh, can't we stay a bit longer?' his wife asked.

'No, we can't. You know how busy it gets Saturdays at Bennie's Bulk-Buy.'

She got up, still holding Ryan's hand like she planned to take it with her. 'It's so good of you to visit him,' she said to us across the bed. 'I hope my lad appreciates what friends he has.'

'Sure he does,' I said, avoiding her eye.

She bent over Bry-Ry and kissed him on the cheek. Then she kissed him on the forehead. Then she kissed him on the hand she was holding. Pete made a little chucking-up noise in my ear. When she'd done all the kissing her lips had time for, Mrs Ryan smiled a goodbye to us and followed

Mr Ryan and little Russell out.

The curtains weren't drawn round the bed today, so I drew the one between us and the nurse's desk. They might come back any time and I had things to say to Ryan in private before we were chucked out.

'Now I want you to listen to me, Ryan,' I said, leaning towards him, but not so close he could reach out and grab me again. 'And I want you to listen good.'

'Yeah, that should win him over,' Pete said.

'Wasn't it friendly enough?'

'Not so much. Give it another go, and lighten up a bit.'

I tried again. Tried to sound friendlier.

'Bryan,' I said. Already it wasn't easy. 'Bry-Ry. I know you blame me for what happened, and believe me if I could go back to that day I'd close my eyes and let you skull me senseless, but I can't, so can we…you know…put it behind us? Forget I was even *near* you that day? Come on, what do you say?'

This was followed by silence, mainly because I'd stopped talking and no one else was. It was Ryan himself who broke the silence. He didn't break it

224

with words, though, or with any other sound from his mouth. He broke it from quite a bit lower down, where all the best raspberries come from.

'I think you got your answer,' Pete said.

I tried again. 'Ryan.' No point being nice if nice didn't work. Straight-talk was the way to handle this. 'Be reasonable, man. We've had our differences, quite a lot of them, but I've never wished you in hospital.'

'You have,' Pete chipped in. 'Dozens of times, I've been there.'

'You've got quite an imagination,' I said, still to Ryan. 'Stampeding horses in the park, angry cloud-cats, little mice on our legs, wa-hoo, impressive. But I could actually do without things like that in my life right now, know what I mean? So how about it? Fainites?'

'What?' said Pete.

'What what?'

'What you just said.'

'What did I just say?'

'Fay something.'

'Fainites?'

'Yeah.'

'It means let's call a truce.'

'I never heard that.'

'One of my grans used to say it. The dead one.'

'Well if it's something a dead grandmother used to say, and it wasn't Ryan's grandmother, why would he know what it means?'

'He doesn't have to know what it means. It's the tone of voice that counts.'

'Your tone of voice says you want to blindfold him and drop him in something deep, thick, and not too brightly-coloured.'

I turned back to the bed. 'Bry-Ry, we've never been best buds, but I really don't deserve to have all this thrown at me. All I did was move. You can't blame me for just *moving*. If everyone got blamed for moving, no one would ever do anything.'

'No one would get out of bed,' Pete said.

'Exactly,' I said. 'Or do anything else either.'

'They wouldn't cross roads,' said Pete.

'No, they wouldn't. So Ryan—'

'Or go to school. But that'd be OK.'

'Yes. Ryan, what I'm saying is—'

'Or get up from the table. Or sit *down* at the table.'

'Or any of that,' I agreed. 'Bry-Ry, I'm asking you to–'

'Or open a door,' Pete said.

'Or open a door. But Ryan, I–'

'Or *close* a door.'

'No. Ryan, we–'

'Or clean their teeth. Or change their pants. Or eat burgers.'

'Absolutely,' I said. 'Ryan '

'Or turn the telly on.'

I turned round. 'Pete.'

'What?'

'Button it.'

'I'm just saying.'

'Well don't, I'm trying to have a serious conversation here.'

'With an unconscious person,' he reminded me.

'If his brain's still working well enough to do all the stuff it's done so far,' I said, 'don't you think it stands a fair chance of hearing me when I speak?'

'It might if brains had ears.'

'It heard a minute ago if that raspberry was an answer.'

'Might just have been a raspberry,' Pete said.

'Nothing to do with ears or brains.'

'Yes, well let's just assume—'

'Why are they called raspberries anyway?'

'Eh?'

'I mean who ever heard an *actual* raspberry make a noise like that? If raspberries blew raspberries, imagine what teatime would be like when everyone has a bowl of them.'

'Garrett,' I said.

'What?'

'Will you just shut it?'

'OK.'

I turned back to Ryan. Would have picked up somewhere near where I left off if there hadn't been another interruption. Not from Pete this time, from a chair on the other side of the bed. A chair that lifted off the ground all by itself, rose to head height, hovered for a few secs like it was getting ready to throw itself at someone, and—

I ducked just in time. The chair whizzed over my head and hit the curtain I'd pulled behind us. The curtain ballooned out and dragged some of its rings off the rail.

We were still gawping at the chair, which had

clattered to the floor, when the two nurses returned.

'What happened?' one of them demanded, rushing to Ryan's bed to check his gadgets and wires.

'Search me,' said Pete, which covered it pretty well for me too.

'I don't remember you two being here,' the other nurse said, picking the chair up.

'We were with his mum and dad,' I said.

'There was only one boy,' the first nurse said. 'A younger boy.'

'We're friends. They said we could come in.'

'Well they shouldn't have done. You'll have to leave.'

It wasn't worth arguing. Wasn't worth staying either, seeing as Ryan's brain had sent a clear message that I'd only just ducked in time.

'You saw that,' I said to Pete on the way downstairs.

'Saw what?'

'The chair lift off the ground and throw itself at me.'

'Yeah.'

'You know that chairs don't usually do that?'

'Yeah. Not usually.'

'Like lemon meringue pie flying round classrooms,' I said.

He grunted. Angie had forced him to say he believed me about the pie, but he hadn't really. Now he had to. A chair that tosses itself over a bed is something even Pete Garrett can't deny.

Chapter Twenty-two

Pete would probably have come in with me, but on the way back his dad phoned to tell him to come and pick up his socks from his bedroom floor like he'd been told a thousand times. Parents, eh?

I didn't feel like ringing my front door bell to ask mine to kindly let me in, which is what I'd had to do all my life so far because I wasn't allowed a key yet.* I went through the back garden instead. The back door key's kept in a hole my dad drilled in the garden gnome's bottom, but I tried the door first to see if it was open. It was. I banged one of Dad's elbows going in because he was right behind it. He swore, told me to watch how I came in, and slung his football scarf round his neck.

'Can you believe it?' Mum said from along the hall. (Our hall runs from back door to front door.) 'He's even going to football on our *anniversary*!'

'It's Saturday afternoon,' Dad replied in a voice that sounded like he'd already said this sixteen

---

* 'You'll get one when you've either proved you're responsible enough or you reach your teens, whichever comes first,' Mum said when I was nine and asked for one, which meant I didn't have long to wait now.

times. 'I always go to football on Saturday afternoon, Peg, you know that.'

'But it's our *anniversary*!' she wailed.

'I *know* it's our anniversary,' he said through his teeth. 'You keep *reminding* me it's our anniversary. But it's not as if it's our first, is it? Far from it. Our anniversaries are lining up like gravestones.'

Mum sniffed. 'I sometimes wonder why you married me.'

'I was young,' he said, pulling his footie supporter's hat on.

'You were twenty-eight.'

'And foolish,' he added.

'I bet you can't even remember our wedding day.'

'Course I can. Remember it like it was yesterday.' He winked at me. 'You know what a terrible day yesterday was.'

'I should have realised what I was in for when you put that banner on the back of the car,' Mum said.

Dad's eyes misted over nostalgically. 'I'd forgotten that.'

'What banner?' I asked.

232

'I was the only person not to see it until we eventually arrived at that dreadful hotel,' Mum said. 'We must have been the laughing stock of the road.'

'What did it say?'

'It said, in the biggest letters imaginable, "Just divorced".'

'It was a joke,' said Dad.

'The whole day was a joke to you, you made that quite clear. My parents weren't amused.'

'Yeah, that was a bonus. Hardly spoke to me for years after that. You know the difference between in-laws and outlaws, Jig?'

'You tell me.'

'Outlaws are wanted.'

'We drove three hundred miles with those words on the car,' Mum said. 'Three hundred miles to the draftiest hotel ever, with the worst food, shocking service, and bunk-beds. Bunk-beds on our wedding night! We couldn't even push them together! And all because your father won a weekend there in a raffle.'

'Another second prize,' Dad muttered.

'Well, thank you *very* much!'

'Not you. The Chinese bike.'

I walked past him, towards Mum. When my parents have a row I try to keep my head down or before long they're shouting at me too because we're a family. I swerved past Mum into the kitchen.

'Anyway,' I heard Dad say in the distance, 'I'm taking you to the musical about the freak in the mask tonight, aren't I? And that overpriced hotel?'

My hand froze as it reached for the Assorted Broken Biscuits tin. Tonight? That was tonight?

'Oh, you're *taking* me, are you?' Mum said.

'All right, it's coming out of the joint purse!' Dad snapped. 'But it's costing an arm, a leg, and two kidneys. Better be worth it, that's all I can say.'

I grabbed a fistful of bickies, went past Mum in the hall again, and plodded upstairs. The parental verbals were still going on down below as I closed the door of my room. Tonight! There was no reason why I should have remembered the wedding anniversary – I was still dribbling soft food down my bib when they signed on the dotted line – but I should have remembered that today was the day they'd booked me into a sleepover at Pete and Angie's. While my parents went to that creepshow with Oliver and Audrey, and afterwards, without

Ollie and Aud, spent the night at the luxury hotel Mum had chosen, I'd be zipped up in a sleeping bag on Garrett's floor.

A minute later I heard Dad slam the door on his way to football. A minute after that my phone rang. Angie.

'Pete says a chair flew your way at the hospital.'

'I thought you weren't talking to me,' I said.

'I didn't say I wasn't talking to you, just to keep away from me.'

'Same thing.'

'It's not. We're talking now, aren't we?'

'Yeah, long-distance.'

'Across the road isn't long-distance.'

'Still not the same room.'

'Tell me about the chair,' she said.

'I thought Pete already told you.'

'I want your version.'

I told her about the chair, my version.

'But why did Pete see it? He hasn't seen anything else.'

'He saw the flying lemon meringue.'

'Well yes, that, but nothing else.'

'I've been thinking about that,' I said. I had too.

'I'm the only one who can see things from Ryan's imagination—'

'The only one?'

'All right, *we're* the only ones who can see things from Ryan's imagination. But anyone can see what his brain does with real things like lemon meringue pie, hospital chairs and revolving doors.'

'Well whatever *else* happens,' she said, 'I don't want any of it coming my way. Until Ryan wakes up and this is over, you keep to your side of the street and I'll keep to mine.'

'Could be a weensy problem with that,' I said.

'What problem?'

I reminded her that her mum and Pete's dad were going out with my parents tonight, and I was sleeping over at hers.

She groaned and hung up.

I was alone again, and immediately worried about what Ryan might do next, and when. I tried to keep my mind off the subject by rubbing last night's brain stuff off my little blackboard and starting another chalk drawing, but I wasn't in the mood. Then I threw myself on my bed to read last week's comic for the fifth time, but I got bored because I knew it by heart already. Then I just lay there with my hands under my head waiting for something to happen. I even invited it so I wouldn't be surprised by it.

'Come on then, Ryan, you dozy turnip, do your stuff.'

Nothing.

After a while I went downstairs. Even my mother's company was better than my own right now.

'Mum, where are you?'

'In here!'

I went through the kitchen. She was on her knees in the garage surrounded by Chinese bike parts.

'What are you doing?'

She looked up. Her eyes were red and puffy. Her lips were two lines so stiff they had trouble parting to let her answer through.

'I'm showing that I'm a better person than *some* people!'

'Pardon?'

She forced her lips further apart to let the words grow a bit.

'I'm showing that I'm a better person than some people.'

'By putting his bike together for him?'

'It's called thinking of others.' She rammed two of the frame sections together like one of them was my father's head. I watched her do some more. She took piece after piece, big pieces and tiny pieces, and fitted them together without a glance at the instructions in Tangerine. My mum's amazing at assembling things. Dad and I can only stand there gaping when she does a flatpack wardrobe.

'Need any help?'

She obviously didn't, but it was her anniversary, felt I should offer. I've never done an I'll-scratch-your-back-if-you-scratch-mine deal with my mum, mainly because she'd never wear it.

'No. Thank you. This is *personal*.'

I trotted to the living room and turned the TV on, flicked channels for a few minutes, found nothing interesting, turned it off again. I went to the window. It all looked so normal out there. The street, the parked cars, the houses. For a minute I almost convinced myself everything *was* normal, but then the sound started. I frowned. Listened harder. Realised.

'Oh, no. Not that. Anything but that.'

I rushed to the door, shut it, put my back against it. But even with the door shut I could hear it. I clapped my hands on my ears. Held them there till my arms got tired. When I lowered them, the sound was still there, but worse, and going on and on and on like it would never end. I thought of turning the TV back on to block it out, but even in such a worthy cause there's just so much I can take of Saturday sport, people competing to cook the best dish, do-it-yourself experts, old cowboy films, and grinning wallies joshing with pint-sized audiences they just *have* to call 'guys'.

There was only one thing for it.

I opened the door and winced across the hall to the kitchen. The awful din got louder and louder. I stumbled to the connecting door with my hands over my ears. I looked into the garage. The Chinese bike almost finished. Just a few more small things to screw in, attach or adjust and it would be done. Mum had obviously forgotten she was mad at Dad because she had her happy face on. Nothing makes my mother happier than putting things together. The only trouble with her when she's happy is…

'Mum!'

The hideous noise went on.

'MUM!'

The noise stopped. She looked up.

'Mother, what's the only way you can hold a tune?'

She looked down at her hands in shame, as well she might, and mumbled something. I cupped my ear.

'Again please?'

She said it again, louder. 'As a hostage.'

'That's right. You might be able to iron shirts, mow grass and put Chinese bikes together, but you cannot *SING*, Mother. So don't!'

I shut the door on her, very firmly.

Chapter Twenty-three

I hung around the kitchen for a bit because I didn't want to be on my own too long and Mum was only a door away. But you can't stay in a kitchen without eating or drinking something, so I took the tin of golden syrup out and dipped a spoon in. I like golden syrup even though I know my teeth will all fall out before I'm twenty-six if I keep eating it neat. At the end of two big, sticky, dripping spoonfuls I felt the skin on my face start to bubble. One more mouthful and an armada of spots would push through and make a firework display of my features. I lidded the tin, but kept the spoon in my mouth till I'd got every last syrupy morsel off it. Only when it was syrup-free did I open the dishwasher to put the spoon in.

Now ordinarily, opening the dishwasher to put a spoon in is an OK thing to do, but I'd been so distracted by my worries that I hadn't noticed the quiet chugging in the background. I shut the door of the thing in a hurry, but just a bit too late.

'Mu-um,' I said, leaning into the garage.

She was fitting the huge bell onto the handlebars of the bike. Once the bell was in place the only thing missing would be the LIGHTNING FLASHER stickers.

She grinned at me. 'What do you think?'

It was a shame to ruin it for her, but I had to.

'Mum, we have a problem.'

'Problem?' she said, buffing the enormous bell with a hanky.

'The dishwasher.'

'What about it?'

'The door opened.'

She stopped buffing. 'The door? The dishwasher door? But the dishwasher's on.' Her eyes slithered down me. 'Jiggy, why are your legs wet?'

'I was standing near when it happened. Whoever loaded it can't have closed it properly. Was it you?'

She leant the bike against the wall. Joined me in the doorway, looked into the kitchen.

'Oh, my God.'

It could have been worse. The floor wasn't

flooded, just kind of swimmy, with a couple of billion bubbles dotted about. But a spot of damp and a bubble or two on a floor are like the end of the world to my mother. She was instantly a mopping, cleaning, grouching machine. I thought of going upstairs to change my leg wear, but if I did that she'd gripe for hours about me always giving her so much washing and ironing to do, so I decided to risk chapped legs and returned to the garage instead. I closed the connecting door to cut her moans off and put the two LIGHTNING FLASHER stickers on the crossbar of the bike. I hoped Dad would appreciate the fact that I'd done this for free.

Once she'd mopped the kitchen floor and told me not to walk on it till it was dry, Mum tried to squeeze the smile back onto her phizog, not because she was happy again but because she thought smiling was what people do on their wedding anniversaries, even when their husband's at football. When Dad came home looking like he'd been dragged backwards across a bumpy field by a fast tractor she even kissed him on the cheek, which she hardly ever does.

'Useless tossers,' he said.

'Who?' Mum asked, helping him out of his scarf.

'The bunch of aliens who've taken over the carcasses of my team.'

'Oh, didn't they do well today then?' Like she cared.

'Do well? They'd have done a better job if they'd gone shopping for tea-towels. Only time they did anything with the ball was when they popped it in their own goal!'

'Well, never mind. I have something to show you that'll cheer you up.'

'*We* have something to show you,' I said.

'Nothing can cheer me up after that fiasco,' Dad said, but Mum took him by the hand and led him like a little kid round the last few puddles on the kitchen floor.

She told him to close his eyes as she opened the door to the garage. She didn't actually say 'Ta-daa,' because even she thinks that's one of the naffest things one human being can say to another, but she did give her wrist a little roll a second after she told him to open his eyes. Dad gaped.

'You put my bike together!'

'I did,' Mum said proudly.

'*We* did,' I said.

We waited for his whoop of delight. We could have waited until the sixth Friday in July, because it didn't happen.

He said: 'I was going to do that after football.'

'Well now you don't have to,' said Mum, still smiling.

'But I was looking *forward* to it.'

The smile shrank. My mother's forehead turned into a cheese-grater. 'I thought you'd be grateful.'

'She did,' I said, backing off. 'I told her not to interfere.'

'It was my prize,' Dad said. 'My prize, not yours. I was going to start on it the moment I got in.'

Mum's eyes flared like matches. 'Start on it? Mel, you hadn't a clue *where* to start.'

'Course I had. I was biding my time to make the most of it. Would've done it in half an hour once I got going.'

'Really. Well, I can take it apart if you like. Then you can put it back together again in half an hour and impress the neighbours when you ride it down the street.'

'No point,' Dad said. 'It's done now.'

He flung himself across the kitchen like someone in high heels, into the hall, out the front door to who-knew-where.

'And a happy anniversary to you too!' Mum shouted after him.

'It's only cos his footie went bums up,' I told her in the silence that followed.

'Well he doesn't have to take it out on *me*,' she said tragically.

I thought of patting her on the shoulder, but I wasn't sure if this was the thing to do and left her to it, went back to my room, hoping Ryan wouldn't throw one of his party tricks while I was on my own in there.*

---

* If you want to know what happened with the bike, here it is. Because Mum put it together Dad never rode it once. Wouldn't even go near it. Spent a lot of time pretending he couldn't see it, hadn't won it, hadn't stared open-mouthed at the instructions in Tangerine. Eventually, Mum – sick of catching her sleeves on the handlebars every time she went into the garage – wheeled it into the garden shed to live with the lawn mower and the spades and forks and things that only she knows how to use. No one ever saw it again because one night the shed was burgled, and the only thing that was stolen was the bike. A genuine Chinese takeaway.

Chapter Twenty-four

Later, when Pete opened their front door to me and my sleeping bag, Angie pounded up to her room. Her mum was in the kitchen, touching up her face in a mirror. 'Mum and Dad say they're ready when you are,' I told her.

She smiled, probably to test her lipstick.

'Hope they're looking forward to it as much as I am.'

'Forward to what?'

'The show.'

'If they are, you wouldn't know it from their silence.'

'Silence?'

'Not speaking to one another.'

'They're not speaking to one another on their anniversary? Why?'

'They didn't say.'

Oliver came trotting down the stairs. I'd hardly ever seen him looking so smart.

'Hi, Jig.'

'What are you going to do with yourselves all evening?' Audrey asked Pete and me.

'I'd suggest Scrabble,' I said, 'but he can't spell it.'

When they'd gone to hook up with my folks, Pete and I went up to his room. Going to someone's room is what you do when you visit their house. Go to their room, play some music, lounge around on the floor or the bed, maybe kill something on the computer, sighing the whole time because none of it's very interesting.

After an hour or so we went downstairs for a change of scenery, raided the kitchen, carried bags, bowls and bottles to the living room. With no Golden Oldies within earsight and Angie shut in her room so she wouldn't be near me, we might have watched something we weren't supposed to on TV, but their satellite dish had fallen down *that very afternoon*, and the only channels that didn't look like a snow blizzard or jerky ghosts were the terrestrials, and there was nothing on them.

'Any good DVDs?'

'Only ones worth watching are locked away,' Pete said.

'Locked in something we could break in to without it showing, or–?'

He shook his head. 'Dad keeps 'em in a special box with a secret code thing on it.'

I looked through the DVD shelves anyway. Needn't have bothered. Most exciting thing there was Bambi, the Director's Cut.

'There's the one that came free with last Sunday's paper,' Pete suggested as a last resort.

He found it. It was in a square cardboard envelope. On the front it said, 'THE CULT CLASSIC, FREE TO ALL READERS!'

'What's a Cult Classic?' I asked.

'Think it means that it's quite old and only three people saw it but they raved about it.'

He turned the envelope over. One of the stills on the back showed this blonde female type with nothing on but a couple of bits of type.

'Could give it a go,' I said.

Pete tossed the disk at the player and we sat back to eat, slurp and watch. The story went like this.

There's this ultra-religious uptight police sergeant from the Scottish mainland who's been sent a letter telling him that a 12-year-old girl's gone missing on a nearby island. He goes to look for her, but everyone on the island says they've never heard of her, which makes the sarge quite suspicious. While he's wandering around that night he sees things that shock him, like couples doing stuff on the grass and a woman without any clothes hugging a gravestone. The sergeant's got himself a room at the pub and he's just getting settled for the night when the blonde female type on the back of the envelope (the landlord's daughter) does this loopy nuddy-wuddy dance in the room next door, slapping the walls and her bare behind and eyeing the camera while she mimes a song played by an invisible band. This drives the copper into a right twitch even though he can't see her.

'This is a spoof, right?' said Pete.

'Either that or the worst film ever made.'

'Can't be. Cult Classic, says so on the packet.'

Next morning the sarge goes to see the Lord of the island, a suntanned smoothy with unbelievable hair who used to play vampires. While they discuss religion, girls wearing leotards run round in circles on the lawn outside, flinging their arms in the air and jumping over a bonfire. Then it's suddenly night again and the sarge thinks he's found the grave of the missing girl and hauls up this ancient coffin with the help of a local gravedigger with a screwy grin and rolling eyes. Inside the coffin they find a dead hare instead of a girl.[*] The sergeant takes the hare to the Lord's pad and throws it on the floor, interrupting the Lord, who's at the piano singing a lively duet with another blonde female type like he wishes this was the musical our parents had gone to see instead of a free DVD about crazy people.

We only carried on watching because this thing had to be seen to be believed. Also, in case any more nuddy stuff occurred. It did. Pete had just freeze-framed a third blonde female type in a little bathtub (with the sergeant apologizing for bursting in on her) when a voice behind us said:

'Typical. The moment the Golden Oldies are out of the way.'

I looked over the back of the couch. Angie.

'I thought you were keeping out of *my* way,'

'I was. But I'm bored.'

'You ought to see this,' Pete said. 'It's the maddest thing ever.'

---

* Hare as in not a rabbit.

'It's a woman in a *bath*,' Angie said.

'Not her, the rest of it.'

'Doesn't look like my sort of thing.'

'It's a Cult Classic,' I informed her.

She came in, but kept her distance like I was contagious. 'What's the story so far?' she asked, parking herself on the arm of a distant chair. We told her. 'Start it again,' she commanded.

'From the beginning?' I said in horror.

'From here'll do.'

Pete thumbed the play button and the sergeant bashed the pub landlord over the head. The landlord had just been getting into a giant Mr Punch outfit, and after the sarge gagged him and tied him to the end of a bed he got into the costume himself. Then, dressed as Mr Punch, with a big hump on his back and a mask with a big nose, he joins the islanders, also in crazy outfits now, dancing in a procession, playing musical instruments, and fighting with wooden swords. A lot of them wear animal heads – cows, bears, goats, that sort of thing. Quite a few have antlers. The Lord of the island leads the procession in a long black wig and a purple dress down to his ankles, dancing like a marionette who's had half his strings cut.

'Is this a joke,' Angie said, 'or the worst film ever made?'

'Cult Classic,' I reminded her.

Then the sergeant, still in the Mr Punch suit, spies the 12 year old girl he's been looking for. She's wearing a white smock, which he thinks means she's going to be sacrificed to the islanders' gods. See, he's learned along the way that the islanders believe that if they kill a person on this day, at a certain time, next season's carrots will be bigger. The sarge grabs the girl and runs through these caves with her, but when they climb up into daylight the Lord of the island and some of the others are waiting for him.

It's only when the girl runs to the Lord for a hug that the policeman realises he might have got something wrong here. The Lord explains in this deep, holy voice (while his unbelievable hair moves romantically in the breeze) that he, the sarge, is the one who's going to be sacrificed. He's been set up. The whole missing girl scenario was a cunning plot to get him to this spot at this very hour.

And this is where the action really started. I don't mean for the characters in this hammy horror of a film, though.

I mean for me.

Suddenly I wasn't on the sofa watching the TV. I was on the other side of the screen, and people in weird costumes and animal heads were standing about, and something was over my face. I pulled the something off my face and stared at the Mr Punch mask. I looked down at myself. I was wearing a baggy clown-type outfit. I felt my back. I had a hump.

I'd become the Scottish police sergeant!

'Jig?'

I looked round. Angie was there too. And…

'Holy loony bins!'

Pete.

It didn't take a genius to realise that Ryan's brain was dumping on me again, or that Angie was there because she'd made the mistake of coming downstairs – but Pete? I must have touched him, grabbed his arm maybe, when I felt myself being dragged into the scene. Like Angie, he was still in his own clothes. Only I was dressed like an oversized refugee from Professor Shanks's puppet show.*

But there had to be some way out of this. Maybe if I could put some space between me and the crazy islanders and the crazy Lord all this would flip back to the TV screen and the three of us would be sitting there picking holes in it again instead of being part of it. I started up a nearby hill, but my way was blocked by this big hairy geezer who knocked me down, picked me up, and carried me back to the Lord of Nutland. Except the Lord of Nutland wasn't himself any more. He still had the suntan and the unbelievable hair, and everyone still called him 'My Lord', but he wore shorts and football boots, and a red shirt with the number eight on it. And he had a different face. The Lord of the island was now...

Bryan Ryan.

---

* See *Neville the Devil*, another terrible tale of woe and misery.

Chapter Twenty-five

Apart from the face and the football gear Ryan was every bit the Lord of the island, acting just as over-the-top as the ex-vampire, even speaking in the same holier-than-thee voice as he informed me that although I was going to be sacrificed I should be happy because I would be reborn as a vegetable.

'Go pickle your brain, Ryan!' I shouted.

If he heard, he didn't let on.

'Behold!' he cried in his new deep voice.

He pointed to the top of the cliff, and this huge model creature, tall as a three storey-house.

A giant origami squirrel.

Four men with flaming torches stood near the squirrel's feet and a wooden ladder led up to a big gap in the squirrel's chest.

'Take him!' Ryan boomed.

The big hairy geezer grabbed my wrists and started pulling me up the slope to the giant origami squirrel. Then the islanders were following us to the beat of a big slow drum, with Ryan in the lead, marching like a tin soldier whose knees need oiling.

'Now just you hang *on* a minute, you lot!'

The slow drum stopped. So did the marchers and the big hairy geezer. So did I, as Angie (who'd shouted this) ran to my side and glared at Lord Ryan of Wacko Island.

'Bry-Ry, you plonker! Stop this right *now*!'

Ryan blinked, and I thought for a sec that he was going to shake himself out of this. But then he gave a little shiver, and he was the Lord again. 'Take her too!' he commanded, and before Angie could do a thing she was being dragged up the hill by the three blonde female types we'd seen earlier from the comfort of a sofa on the Brook Farm Estate.

We were at the foot of the ladder that stood against the giant origami squirrel when Pete came to the rescue for the second time that day. I don't know what had kept him – probably trying to get his graffiti-covered head round the scene – but suddenly there he was, at the squirrel's feet. And he was armed. With a set of antlers.

'The first person to move gets spiked!' he shouted.

257

The big hairy geezer and the three blonde female types froze, but one of the islanders following us stepped out of line and raised a hand to his ear.

'What was that? I'm a wee bit hard of hearing!'

And Pete, because he'd threatened the first person to move, charged down the hill at the deaf person, waving the antlers.

Berk.

Half the islanders lurched sideways as he passed, knocked the antlers out of his hands, hauled him back to us.

While Pete was being dragged back up the hill, the big hairy geezer threw me over his shoulder and headed up the ladder. When we reached the top he dumped me in the gap in the squirrel's chest and went down again. While he was gone I tested the floor. It might only have been paper, but it was the strongest origami I'd ever seen. I tried kicking it with my heel. It didn't tear. I tried jumping on it. Didn't even dent.

Pete came up the same way I had, over the big hairy geezer's shoulder. The BHG dropped him beside me and went down once more.

'What happens now?' Pete said, getting to his feet.

'I expect he'll bring Angie up.'

'After that.'

'Dunno. Can't wait to find out.'

'I can.'

Angie kicked and fought all the way up, but it didn't do her any good. When she'd been put in with us, the big hairy geezer pulled this gate down from somewhere overhead. The bars of the gate weren't made of paper. They were black, sort of sticky, like...

'Liquorice?' Angie said.

'No, can't be.'

She licked one of the bars, and nodded. 'Liquorice.'

I remembered something about Ryan. He almost always had a bag of liquorice bootlaces in his pocket. I mentioned this.

'Makes sense if all this is out of his imagination,' Angie said.

'What are you saying?'

'I'm saying it makes sense if all this is out of his imagination.'

'I mean what do you mean?'

'I mean he probably would include things he knows or likes in a scenario he's made up.'

'He didn't make it up, it's a Cult Classic.'

'Might have started as a Cult Classic, but then his brain took over, yanked us into the story, changed a few things around, and gave the Lord of the island his own face and soccer gear.'

'If that's right,' I said, 'the story might have turned out differently on the DVD. For instance, the Scottish sergeant might not have been popped into a giant origami squirrel.'

'Squirrel?' said Pete. 'I thought it was a monkey.'

'No. Squirrel. Definitely a squirrel.'

'The origami is a puzzle,' Angie said.

'Maybe not,' I said. 'Maybe when Ryan's at home he sits around with his little brother making origami animals.'

'Little brother?'

'Turns out he's got one. Name's...what was it, Pete?'

'Don't remember. Don't care. All I know is—'

'What's that smell?' Angie blurted.

We sniffed. Something burning. We looked down. Smoke, leaking through the floor.

'I knew they were taking a chance standing that close with those torches,' I said.

'It didn't occur to you that that might be what the torches were for?' said Angie. 'To light the squirrel?'

'Um…' It hadn't.

'You're going to be sacrificed, remember. That probably didn't mean putting you up for auction on eBay.'

I stared at the smoke curling round my ankles.

'You mean…?'

'I mean we have to act,' Angie said. 'Find some way out of here.'

We started punching the paper walls to try and break through, but like the floor they weren't made of standard origami. You couldn't make holes in them, rip them, even make a crease.

'Listen,' said Pete suddenly.

'Don't tell me,' I said. 'You've got a cunning plan to get us out of here.'

'No,' he said. 'Listen.'

We listened.

'Singing,' said Angie.

We peered through the sticky liquorice bars. Ryan and dozens of islanders stood in a row on the headland below, gazing up at us, swinging their arms from side to side, and warbling some cheerful ditty about summer a'coming in while flames licked the paper floor under our feet. Any minute now they'd be licking us too.

'We're doomed,' said Pete.

'Maybe the paper floor won't burn,' I said hopefully.

'Maybe it will.'

'We're forgetting something,' Angie said.

'What's that?' I said. 'How to smile?'

'We're forgetting that this isn't real.'

'Feels pretty real to me.'

'Course it does. It's meant to. But Ryan's brain's planted all this in our minds. Nothing that's happening can harm us.'

'I'll try and remember that as I burn to a crisp,' I said.

But maybe because she'd said it and it was true, when the floor gave way a second later we didn't plunge screaming into fire and smoke. We plunged screaming onto...

The living room sofa.

And a second after that the door behind us opened.

'Hello, you three. Having a good evening?'

Audrey and Oliver, back from the show. Must have heard our screams as they opened the front door, taken them for squeals of pleasure at something on the box.

I glanced at the TV. The credits of the Cult Classic were rolling. No mention of us as stars.

Chapter Twenty-six

When the three of us were alone again and the TV was off, Pete thumped my arm. Hard.

'Ow! What was that for?'

'What was it for? What do you *think* it was for?'

I rubbed my bicep. 'You can't blame me for all that. I didn't make it happen.'

'Oh no? Who did then?'

'Well...Ryan.'

'Ryan's out to get you because you dodged his head and parked him in hospital, and we've been dragged along for the ride as usual, so it's your fault. Every lousy bit of it.'

To make sure I got the gist of his argument he thumped my other arm. Ordinarily I'd have thumped him back for the second one, if not the first, or maybe thrown myself at him and pummelled him to the carpet, but I had to admit he'd got a point.

'OK, I said, holding my hands up to calm him

down. 'OK, OK, OK. The thing is, how do we make sure Ryan doesn't do something else?'

'I don't want to talk about Ryan,' Pete said. 'I don't want to talk about him, think about him, hear his name. I want to forget he ever existed.' He scowled at me. 'And you, you're sleeping in the bathroom.'

'He can't sleep in the bathroom,' said Angie. 'Someone might want to use it in the night.'

'He can have the bath, draw the shower curtain across, no one'll know he's there.'

She made a don't-mess-with-me face. 'He is *not* sleeping in the bathroom.'

'Well, I don't want him anywhere near me in case something else happens and I can't doze through it.'

'Now you know why I wanted to keep my distance from him.'

'O-o-o-o-oh yes!'

I sighed. 'There were times, not so long ago, when we did everything as a team. If one of us was in a spot of bother the other two didn't slam the door in their face. Shoulder-to-shoulder, back-to-back, toe-to-toe, that was us. One for all, no question.'

'Yeah, well some things you grow out of,' Pete said. 'I have better things to do than follow you around with a shovel.'

'You want out of the Musketeers?' I asked him.

There was a long silence. Then: 'Maybe it's time.'

I looked at Angie. 'And you?'

Another long silence. Then: 'I'll give it a bit longer.'

This was a sad day. Sad night. But...

'Can't we just stick it out till this is over?' I whined pathetically.

'Stick with you, you mean,' said Pete.

'Yes. Please?'

Looooong silence. Then: 'Well...'

'Is that a yes?'

'No, it's a well.'

'So what does it mean?'

'Means I'll think about it.'

'How long for? Till Ryan's done his absolute worst and turned me into a quivering shadow of my former self?'

'You don't think tonight was his absolute worst?' Angie asked.

'Dunno. Have to wait and see. Pete.'

'What?'

I offered him my hand. Time for the secret handshake of solidarity.

'What's that?' he said.

'My hand. For the secret handshake of solidarity.'

'What secret handshake of solidarity?'

'The one we've been using since we were six.'

'I don't remember a secret handshake of solidarity.'

'Course you do. We've used it quite often, haven't we, Ange?'

'Have we?' she said.

I gave up. The secret handshake of solidarity was even more secret than I thought.

I did sleep on Pete's floor that night, but he pretended I wasn't there by huddling under his duvet the whole time and not speaking. Usually when I stay at Pete's, or he stays at mine, we sit up half the night talking about nothing much because talking about nothing much isn't something we can do at night normally. Not that night though. He didn't want anything to do with me that night.

Pete needn't have worried. Nothing happened all

night, though I woke a couple of times from weird dreams I immediately forgot. But something must have come out of those dreams because when I woke the last time, in the morning, there was an idea in my head that hadn't been there before. I told the others about it over breakfast.

'Pay Mrs Ryan a visit?' Angie said. 'What good'll that do?'

'Could change everything,' I said. 'I've tried getting through to Bry-Ry and failed, but his mum seems to think a lot of him for some reason, so maybe he thinks a lot of her. My thought is that if I'm ultra-nice to her she might pass it on to him in his sleep next time she visits. If she does, it might sink in to his rotten brain that I'm not such a bad person after all and leave me alone. Leave *us* alone. Will you come with me?'

Pete wasn't keen, but Angie persuaded him with one of her threats, and he reached for the woolly bobble hat he'd worn on his first day as a totally bald person.

'I thought that one made your head itch,' I said.

'It does, but I'll put up with. Don't feel such a prat in this one.'

268

'Really?'

'Yeah, really.'

'I think your hair's started to grow back.'

He peered in the hall mirror. 'You think?'

'Definitely. Another month and no one'll know your head was vandalised by hooligans who can't spell and don't know where apostrophes go.'

We left the house.

The Ryans live on the Honeybun Estate, which is about half a brick's throw from Borderline Way, the street Angie, Pete and I grew up in.* Honeybun isn't like the Brook Farm Estate, where we live now. It's one of the old ones, one of the rough ones, the kind you walk through with your eyes down so you don't swap gazes with the residents – specially the kids, in case they stop peeing against the walls they've just spray-painted and come at you with bicycle chains.

Fortunately, the house we wanted was on the edge of the estate – one of the ones backing onto the school playing field – so we didn't have long to worry about rocket grenades being launched at us from bedroom windows. It had never occurred to me before, but Ryan's house overlooking the

---

* All the Borderline Way houses were pulled down recently to make way for a shelter for the homeless.

school might be why he shows off so much on the footie pitch: in case his family's watching from one of the windows.

Mrs Ryan was stuffing weeds into a brown wheelie bin as we sauntered up to her front gate.

'Oh, hello!' she said, breaking into a huge smile. 'Caught me tidying the garden. It certainly needs it. My Joe used to do it, but he put his back out and it just got left and left until I couldn't stand it. He's at the snooker club today, the Sunday Tournament, so I thought I'd see what I could do in his absence. Who's this?'

I told her who Angie was and Mrs Ryan removed her gardening gloves, opened the gate and took her hand. She didn't shake it, just took it – and held on to it. She obviously liked holding people's hands.

'Have you heard how Bryan is today?' Angie asked. It just rolls off her silken tongue, that sort of talk.

'Oh, you know, he's muddling through.'

'What's the prognosis?'

Our heads swivelled. The *prognosis*? What sort of word was that for a girl who wasn't even in her teens yet?

Mrs Ryan folded Angie's arm into her own and headed up the path with it. 'They say he could come out of it at any time or he could stay that way for weeks, months even. There's no telling. You will come in, all of you, won't you? I have a nice chocolate cake with a buttercream filling.'

Pete pushed past me to beat me into the house.

In the hallway Mrs Ryan stepped out of her gardening boots and closed the door. It was very tidy inside, bright and cheerful, not at all like you'd expect a Honeybun house to be. She showed us into the living room, an old-fashioned sort of room, but kind of nice, like her. There were framed photos all over the place, including some of Bry-Ry when he was younger, in school uniform with a tooth missing, or on holiday, or with really ancient Golden Oldies who I suppose were his grandparents. Quite a shock, that room. Much too cosy for the Ryan I knew. He might have sat in here with a tea tray on his knees, watching something on the box like I do with my parents at weekends. I'd never thought of Ryan having an ordinary family life. Nor had Pete and Angie. We talked about this in whispery voices, sitting in a row on the couch while Mrs Ryan did stuff in the kitchen. When she came back she was pushing one of those trolleys with upper and lower floors.

'I wasn't sure what you'd like to drink,' she said, 'so I brought limeade, orange juice and chocolate milk. It's a bit early for this sort of thing, but it's not every day friends of my boy pay a visit...'

She stopped. A small person had appeared in the doorway. Her other son, the one with the rust-coloured spiky hair. He was holding a tabby cat in his arms. Another cat, a black one with a white bib, twined itself around his ankles.

'Russell, look, Bryan's friends are here.'

Ryan's little brother didn't seem any more pleased to see me than he had at the hospital. The way he *looked* at me!

'Come and have some cake with us,' Mrs Ryan said. 'Special elevenses in honour of our guests.'

But he didn't come in. He stayed in the doorway, staring at me, hardly blinking, stroking the cat. The tabby also stared at me, and so did the one on the floor, like they were picking up some sort of anti-McCue vibe. I remembered the cloud cats in the park. Ryan's brain must have based them on these two.

'Russ. Be polite now.'

The kid can't have been in the mood for polite because he span round and went upstairs without a word, carrying the tabby, followed by the other cat.

'He's shy,' Mrs Ryan explained as she heaped slices of cake onto three plates. 'And still very upset. Help yourselves to the drinks.'

'Upset?' Angie said, taking a loaded plate.

'Yes. It's hit him hard. He worships his big brother.'

'He worships *Ryan*?' I said. It was out before I could stop it. Angie gave me one her best withering looks. 'I mean Bryan,' I said. It wasn't easy, being nice about my arch-enemy.

'Oh yes,' Mrs R said. 'Thinks the world of him, he does. It goes back to when Russ was little. He...'

She went to the door and pushed it to. Dropped her voice to say the next bit.

'He doesn't speak, you know.'

'Doesn't speak?' said Angie.

'Hasn't said a word since he was five.'

'Really?'

273

'The specialists say there's no reason for him not to talk, but he refuses to even try. It was the accident. Not Bryan's accident, but it could have been as bad. Could have been worse. Much worse. Russell might have died if not for our Bry.'

'What happened?'

This was Pete. Suddenly he was interested in more than chocolate cake. Near-death experiences and other disasters often switch a light on in his eyeballs. While the rest of us put our hands to our cheeks and say, 'Oh, but that's *awful*,' Pete gets all attentive. Leans forward. Wants every last detail.

Mrs Ryan sat herself down in the armchair facing us. She hadn't brought a plate in for herself, or anything to drink. She'd just wanted us to have something.

'Russell's always been curious about how things work,' she said. 'From the moment he could crawl he was into things. When he was five he started asking questions about electricity. We told him you had to be careful with it, but that can't have been good enough for him because one Saturday morning Bryan came out of the bathroom as Russ was about to put one of my hairpins in a plug

274

socket on the landing. He shouted at him not to do it, but Russell just grinned, and when Bry ran to pull him away Russell stuck the pin in. I heard their cries from the kitchen and shot upstairs, found them twitching together in this fidgety blue light.' There was a sob in her voice as she said the next bit. 'I'm so thankful. I could have lost both my boys in a minute. I am so *thankful.*'

'What happened then?' Angie asked.

'They were in hospital for three days, side by side, sleeping mostly while their bodies recovered from the shock. We had their beds pushed together and I hardly left them the whole time. (Joe visited two or three times too, he was very good.) Quite often, in his sleep, Russell's hand would reach over and take hold of Bryan's, like he was looking after him, making sure he was all right. It's been like that ever since. Russell's the young one, but when you see them together it's like *he's* the older brother. He gets quite upset if anything happens to Bry — when he gets injured while playing one of his rough games, for instance, or if he hears about something bad that's happened to him at school.'

I cleared my throat. 'Um...' Six eyes turned to me.

'Was Russell at school last week?'

'At school?' Mrs Ryan said. 'Well yes, of course. 'Except for Wednesday. One of those teacher training days. We were told in advance, but some of us have to work, or be at the snooker hall exercising our poorly backs, so the youngsters are in the house on their own. It's not right.'

So now I knew why Russell kept giving me the bad eye. He must have been watching from the house last Wednesday when his brother lobbed his head at me. Saw me dodge out of the way. Blamed me for Ryan being in hospital.

We'd gobbled our cake and said how good it was, and were swapping, 'have-we-been-nice-enough-to-her-to-go-now?' glances when Mrs Ryan said:

'Would you like to see Bryan's room?'

We wanted to say, 'Well actually, that's just about the last room in the solar system we want to see,' but what two of us said was, 'That'd be great,' while the third muttered, 'In a pig's knacker' so quietly that only I heard it.

We went upstairs. At the top and along a bit, Mrs R pushed a door back.

'Here we are.'

We went in. Stood there like people who've come to look at a house they have no intention of buying. This room was very Ryan. He had his own TV with built-in DVD player (the camouflaged one I'd seen him looking at in Turpin's – maybe he'd been saving up for it). There were a couple of army posters on the walls, but there were a lot more football posters, plus photos and cartoons of players. There were also lots of little model footballers with their legs or arms in the air, and over to one side there was one of those soccer games with a green table that you move the little players around on. And the wallpaper pattern was...

'He likes football, doesn't he?' I said.

'Oh yes, my Bry likes his football.' Mrs R smiled lovingly at the duvet, which, surprise-surprise, was in the colours of his favourite team. 'That's where he sleeps.'

'Get away,' Pete said, in a never-have-guessed-it voice.

It was so neat, that bed, even neater than mine when my mum makes it, not a crease anywhere, as if Mrs Ryan had made it with special care after her son was taken to hospital and meant it to stay that way forever. Four candles in big wooden holders at the corners and it would have looked like a shrine.

'Eeeergh,' Pete said suddenly.

Three heads turned in surprise. 'Eeeergh' is the sort of thing you say when you've seen something that turns your stomach, not what you say when you're a guest in someone's house. But as it happened, this was an 'Eeeergh' that Pete had good reason for. Over in the corner was a glass tank, the kind you put fish in, though there weren't any fish in this one. It had a blue plastic lid with holes in it so the things inside could breathe but not get out. The things inside were snails, worms and slugs. Two of the slugs were climbing the side of the tank that faced us, showing us their horrible smooth bellies as they slithered up.

Mrs Ryan giggled at our faces. Her big blue eyes shone.

'They're Russell's. Garden creatures are one of his little interests. Another is movies. He watches movies for hours. All sorts of movies. He was watching that one about the gladiator the other day. Played his favourite scenes over and over.

278

He loves horses too,' she added.

'Horses?' I said.

'Mad about them. Always drawing them.'

She pointed to a batch of horse drawings stuck on Ryan's headboard. Small drawings, brightly coloured.

'He does them for his brother,' Mrs Ryan said fondly. 'He'd probably draw the snails and things as well, but he knows Bry prefers the horses.'

Either he'd heard himself being talked about or he didn't want to miss anything, but suddenly Russell was in that doorway too. The cats weren't with him this time. His mum reached for him.

'He's been sleeping in here since the accident. On the floor.' She nodded at a rolled-up sleeping bag beside the bed.

'I did that last night,' I said brightly.

'Did what?'

'Slept on the floor in a sleeping bag.' She looked puzzled. 'Not this floor,' I explained, wishing I hadn't mentioned it.

Angie asked why Russell was sleeping here and Mrs R pulled him close. 'He misses his big brother, don't you, precious?'

Precious didn't look up at her, or smile sweetly like little kids usually do when they're hugged. He squirmed away and went to the football table while she told us more about how close he and his brother were. I was the only one watching when Russell stood one of the little players against a goalpost and made another one dive at him, slowly, head-first. He checked to make sure I was looking as he did this. Just before the players collided, he made the one at the goalpost step aside, so the diving one banged his head on the post. Then he dropped that one and made the other one do a jolly little dance around him.

'I sometimes think they're psychic,' Mrs Ryan was saying. 'Bryan starts to say something and Russell nods, like he's ahead of him. During the week before the football accident they were conducting these mind-reading experiments. Bry said it was amazing the way Russell could get inside his head. He's very bright, our little chap. Wants to be a scientist like that Stephen Dawkins when he grows up, don't you, R–'

'Oh!'

This was Angie. She was holding a cardboard envelope I never wanted to see again. Russell went to the TV and sprang the DVD tray. He took the envelope from Angie and dropped the disk in, looking at me as he did it, like he wanted me to see this too.

'We should go,' Pete said. He'd been standing by the door making hints with his eyes almost since we came up here.

'We should,' said Angie. 'Our parents'll be wondering where we've got to.'

She followed Pete out. Mrs R went next. As I was going I heard a small throat clearing behind me. I looked round. Russell was holding out a folded piece of paper.

'What's that?'

He jerked his hand forward and I seemed to hear a voice in my head saying 'Take it!' I took it. I would have opened it and looked at it, but Russell closed my hand over it. As he touched me I felt a tingle like a small electric shock.

Something pinged in my brain.

I shoved the note in my pocket and went after the others in a hurry. I thought Russell would stay in the room, but he followed me, two stairs behind. The hair stood up on the back of my neck all the way down.

In the hall, Pete was holding the front door handle impatiently while Angie thanked Mrs Ryan for the refreshments and guided tour. We were about to leave when Mrs R said:

'What is it, dear?'

She was looking at Russell. He'd moved along the hall, was standing half way to the back door.

'He seems to think you can get home quicker across the playing field,' Mrs Ryan said.

I don't know how she could tell that's what he meant, but it was true. If we went over the playing field and hopped across the allotments on the other side, we could be on our estate in under fifteen minutes. Take about twenty-five the usual way.

'How does he know that?' Angie asked.

'Perhaps Bryan's told him where you live, you being such friends,' Mrs Ryan said. 'But I'm not sure you're allowed on school premises at weekends...'

Russell already had the back door open. His eyes were on me again. That weird little kid, who'd almost died when an electric current zipped through him at the age of five and who'd never spoken since, was telling me, with his staring eyes, that we had to leave by that door.

'Someone's playing there,' Pete said, peering along the hall.

The field was just over the back garden, the other side of a metre-high fence. Four bald boys were kicking footballs around out there. Ecjit Atkins and his pals.

'Oh, well, I suppose if *some* are there...' Mrs Ryan said.

Russell ran on ahead and waited for us to join him at a small garden shed that stood against the fence. Mrs Ryan stayed on the back step as we went after him. We expected to have to climb the fence, but Russell opened the shed door and pointed inside. There were all the usual tools in there, and it whiffed of cobwebs and varnish and stuff, and we had no idea what he was showing us until he went in and slid a panel in the wall aside. There was no fence on the other side of the panel, just the green grass of the playing field. Pete ducked through and Angie followed him. As I stooped to take my turn Russell gave me a farewell shove – and another little shock. The panel in the side of the shed closed behind me.

I was back where all this had started four days earlier.

Chapter Twenty-seven

Atkins and his skinhead buds were still kicking balls about in the distance. Normal kids might play with one ball at a time, but the Atkins gang had two, which made it hard for them to decide which one to go for, so they kicked whichever was nearest, then hared after the other. As well as kicking them, they threw them and ran with them in their arms. They also thumped one another quite a bit, and tripped one another up, bellowing the whole time.

'Well, let's hope it worked,' Angie said as we started across the field.

'Hope what worked?' I said.

'The being nice to mum act.'

'She's hard not to be nice to.'

'Yeah, but let's hope she passes the news on to Ryan.'

'I'm not sure that it matters.'

'Not sure it matters? Wasn't that what we went there for?'

'Well, it *was*, but...'

'But what?'

I looked at each of them in turn. 'Did you two miss all that?'

'All what?' said Pete.

'You did, didn't you?'

'Oi, you free, wot yoo doin' 'ere then?'

Atkins had spotted us.

'Don't you know this field's out of bounds?' Angie shouted.

Eejit kicked the nearest ball into his nearest bud's squashies. 'Yer, course, why'd ya fink we're 'ere?'

'The little brother,' I said as the Baldy Boys went back to chasing one another and bellowing. 'Russell. He was watching the same DVD as us last night. Probably at the same time.'

'Yes, quite a coincidence, that,' Angie said.

'Maybe not such a coincidence.'

'What else could it be?'

'I think he's got more going for him than he lets on.'

'Well I don't know what. The poor kid can't speak.'

'I think he could if he wanted to.'

'Where'd you get that from?'

'A little voice in my head. Maybe sticking the hairpin in that socket made him not *want* to speak any more. Or need to. His mother seems to know what he means without him saying a word.'

'That's because she's his mother,' Angie said.

'Maybe. But I bet big brother does too.'

'Well, Ryan and the kid both had 5000 bolts up 'em,' Pete said.

'Accounts for Bry-Ry's electrifying personality,' said Angie.

I stopped walking. They stopped too.

'You don't get it, do you?'

'Get what?' said Pete.

'I'm no longer sure that it's Bryan Ryan who's been dumping on me since he cracked his head on that goalpost.' I pointed to it in case they hadn't realised where we were. 'I think it's *Russell* Ryan.'

'Uh?' said Pete.

Angie frowned. 'But it's not Russell who's in hospital.'

'No. If he was, he probably wouldn't be able to do any of the stuff we've been blaming his brother for.'

'Jig, that boy can't be much more than eight years old.'

'Mozart was playing the guitar when he was three,' I said.

'I think it was four. And the harpsichord.'

'What I'm saying is, Russell's a young kid whose been at the spiky end of a powerful electric charge that juiced something in his brain. Gave him the power to fling lemon meringue about, throw chairs, spin revolving doors, and, once a connection's been made to them, put images in people's heads.'

'And sense when they're watching a Cult Classic and make them appear in an alternative version of it?' said Pete.

'Why not? He and his brother are already connected, have been since the hairpin in the socket event, and since last Wednesday Russell's been connected to me too, through Bry-Ry.'

'How's that then?'

'Just after he took that dive Ryan gripped my

ankle. Even though he was face down in the grass the idea of hurting me was still in his mind. I felt a tingle like a small electric shock when he grabbed me — and I got a shock just like it, twice, from Russell back there at the house.'

'You didn't say,' Angie said.

'I'm saying now. I think that when Ryan took hold of my ankle the hostile charge he put into me automatically connected me to Russell. Then, at the hospital the following night, Russell picked up on my terrible footballer jibe and got Bry-Ry to grip my hand in his sleep — which made the connection between us even stronger. It's all been Russell.'

'You sound pretty sure of this now,' Angie said.

I glanced back at the house. A small spiky head was watching us from an upstairs window of the Ryans' house.

'Getting surer by the minute.'

'But why would Russ have it in for you? It's his brother who's in hospital, not him.'

'Exactly. The brother he looks up to. The brother who probably saved his life that day on the landing by taking some of the electrical charge. The brother whose enemies he thinks of as his enemies.'

'You and Ryan have always been enemies and nothing like this ever happened before,' Pete said.

'I've never put him in hospital before.'

'You *said* you didn't this time.'

'I didn't, but it might have looked like I did from there—' they glanced at the little head in the window '—and that I was thrilled to bits about it.'

'You think he saw what happened?' Angie said.

'I know he did. Except what he saw and what actually occurred weren't quite the same thing. He thought I was dancing a joyful jig when Bry-Ry hit the turf. I wasn't dancing, I was doing the standard jig that I can't help when things get a bit heavy.'

'So you believe the kid's been putting you through all this to pay you back for seeming to enjoy what you didn't do to his lousy brother?' Pete said.

'Right. I'm guessing that the first thing, the flying lemon meringue, was an experiment. When he found he could do stuff like that, he had a go at stampeding horses and the rest, making sure that I'd think it was his brother getting back at me. He even made an image of Bry-Ry appear in my bedroom a couple of times. Fed his voice into my head too. Oh, hang on, he gave me something.'

I fished in my pocket for the piece of paper Russell had made me take. I unfolded it. This was it.

'Isn't that some Golden Oldie pop group?' Pete asked.

'Think so,' I said.

'Maybe his mum likes them,' said Angie.

'Why would he want me to know the name of a pop group his mum likes?'

'Well, maybe he—'

Slither-slither-skwoosh-skwersh-slither-slither.

We turned to see what the peculiar noise was, and why a shadow had just fallen over us. Atkins and his gang larking about, I thought, getting ready to give them an earful.

But it wasn't Atkins and his gang. It was nothing like Atkins and his gang. Between us and them, quite a bit too close for comfort, was an enormous creature with rubbery brown skin and eyes on stalks. There were two more stalks lower down, tentacles like skinny elephant trunks that made little sniffy sounds as if they were trying to decide if we used deodorant. Between these two tentacles a wide slit of a mouth dribbled oily-looking stuff, making a pool of drool.

It was a slug.

The biggest, ugliest, slimiest slug you could ever hope not to meet outside of a nightmare.

I glanced back at the house. Little Russell waved at me from the window.

Shlurrrp.

I looked back at the humungerungerous slug.

'Where's Pete?'

'In there,' Angie said in a small shocked voice.

She pointed a shaky finger at the slug's mouth. There was a bubble between where the lips would be if it had any.

'Pete's in there?'

'Yes.'

'How?'

'One of those tentacle things lifted him up and tossed him in.'

'What are we gonna do?' I said.

292

'I'll tell you what we're gonna do,' she replied. 'We're gonna get out of here while we can.'

'What about Pete?'

'Pete can look after himself.'

'In a slug's mouth? I wouldn't be too sure about that.'

'What do you want us to do, go in after him?'

'You're right,' I said. 'Let's get outta here.'

And we would have if the two ground-floor tentacles hadn't slapped against our chests and held us like bits of carpet on the end of vacuum cleaner tubes. Next thing we knew we were off our feet and being carried towards the huge, wide, drooly mouth.

Chapter Twenty-eight

It was one of those moments when everything happens at the speed of light but seems to happen at the speed of custard. Way above us the stalky eyes stared down, obviously not wanting to miss a second as we were whisked through the air. I seem to remember saying something like 'Woooooooooh!' as we plunged into the bubble on the slug's mouth. I think Angie said something similar, but I didn't care enough to take out a pen and write it on my hand.*

'Hey, watch where you're going!'

Pete. We'd crashed into him on the other side. The mouth closed instantly. It was very dark in there.

'I can't see a thing,' Angie said.

'Do you want to?' I asked.

'No, not really.'

Plurpp.

'Something dropped on my head,' said Pete.

---

* Flying into that mouth without a passport was not one of the great trips of my life if you want to know, though there's a chance that I'll still be jerking up in bed, slug-eyed from dreaming of it, when I'm eighty.

Plurpp.

'And mine,' I said.

Plurpp.

'And mine,' said Angie.

Our eyes strained to get used to the darkness. See what had plurpped on us.

Plurpp. Plurpp. Plurpp.

More. This time on our upturned faces.

'What do you think it is?' I asked.

'Dunno,' said Angie. 'Saliva?'

One of us said 'Ick!', and we stepped smartly out of range while whipping out our handkerchiefs.

'Here's a thought,' Pete said when there was more sluggy saliva on our hankies than on us. 'A slug's is a sort of animal, right?'

We agreed that a slug was probably a sort of animal.

'And animals swallow what goes in their mouths, yes?'

'Yes…'

'Well maybe we should feel around for something to hold on to so we don't go any further.'

'Go further?' I said.

'Into the stomach.'

'Something to hold on to?'

'Well, a handle, say. Three handles if they're going begging.'

'That's dim even by your standards, Garrett,' Angie said. 'Why would slugs have handles fitted in their mouths?'

Before he could think of an answer the slug's mouth opened again to let something else in.

A giant worm.

It was a very plump, galumphing, slow-slithering worm, grey and oily-looking in the light from the gap it was coming through. The thought of being touched by it made us all jump back out of its way. Jumping back without looking to see what was behind us turned out to be a less than good move. Pete and Angie ended up against the back of the slug's mouth, but I'd backed into the corner where the throat began, and the floor was especially slippery there. I reached for the nearest thing to stop myself going down the throat, but the nearest thing was Angie's arm and my grab made her feet slip too, and she started to come with me. To try and stop *herself*, she grabbed the nearest thing to her – Pete's arm – but her grab made his

296

feet skid as well, so we went round the corner together, all three of us. Round it and beyond, hurtling down this long, dark, bumpy tunnel, head-over-heels, tumbling and tumbling, until we came out the other end and sat up in something squelchy.

We were in the slug's stomach.

We hauled ourselves out of the something squelchy and stood up. Looked around. As you might expect, the slug's stomach was much bigger than its mouth. It was a deepish sort of purple, and the walls were running with this thick green gunge like the stuff that comes out of a nose with bad catarrh. We could see the colours because of the light from these little flaps all around that opened and closed and went pup-pup-pup.

'Air holes,' said Angie.

'Who?' I said.

'No, those things. I think they let air in and out.'

'Isn't that what the mouth's for?'

'Maybe this is extra, like nostrils. I didn't see any nostrils before we came in, did you?'

'No.'

The slug's stomach reminded me of the inside of

a roast chicken that hasn't been cleaned out yet. We were the only human visitors, but there were bits of bushes, patches of grass, clumps of fungus, heaps of rotting vegetables, and lots of other stuff I could've done without seeing. There were also quite a few dead insects (larger than normal and twice as horrible) and a couple of live snails as big as taxis that moved slowly round the edge, watching us from a safe distance with *their* stalky eyes. Standing in the middle of all that, I had a sudden longing to be in Face-Ache Dakin's maths class.

The worst thing of all wasn't what you could see, though. It was what you could smell. If you've never been in a giant slug's stomach you might have trouble imagining that smell. I'm going to have trouble describing it, but I'll try. Think of climbing into a rubbish bin that hasn't been emptied for a year. You burrow right down and stick your head in the big heap of leftover food at the very bottom that's gone all mouldy and slimy. Now imagine sniffing that mess through the nostril equivalent of an ear trumpet so that it smells a hundred and one times worse than it is. Now you're half way to understanding what it smells like in a giant slug's stomach.

'What we have to remember,' Angie said from deep inside her hands, 'is that this isn't real.'

'Seems real enough to me,' said Pete from deep inside his.

'Yes, but whoever heard of a slug this big? I bet if we closed our eyes and focussed our minds on the playing field without the slug, when we opened them again we'd be back on dry grass watching Atkins and his mob playing with their balls.'

'It's worth a try,' I said.

Pete agreed, and we closed our eyes and focussed our minds on the playing field without a giant slug.

'Can we open 'em yet?' Pete said after a while.

'We're still here,' I said. 'The stink's as bad as ever. And we can't hear Atkins and Co.'

'Give it a bit longer,' Angie said.

We gave it a bit longer.

'Still pongs,' said Pete after another while.

'It's not working,' I said.

'No,' said Angie.

We opened our eyes. We were still in the slug's stomach.

Shhhhlopp.

'Uh?'

Something had dripped onto the top of our heads. We looked up. We were standing under a huge dripping lump, like an oversized boil that's just burst. If it *was* a boil, it meant that we were covered in pus.

Slug pus.

Well of course, the first thing we did when this thought occurred was step well back and shudder horribly. The second thing was swab our faces with our hankies. Unfortunately our hankies were already wet from the slug's saliva, so we were soon wiping as much pus on as we wiped off.

'The grass!' Angie cried

She pounced on the grass lying in clumps on the stomach floor. So did Pete and I, snatching clump after clump, wiping our heads like maniacs. We were so busy wiping that we didn't notice the something huge that shlumped out of the throat behind us. We noticed when it smacked us face down in a pool of green slime we'd been planning to avoid, though.

Our friend the giant worm had joined us.

The worm didn't seem too bothered that we were the only human faces in that part of the world, probably because those faces were deep in the slime pool it was slithering over. To the worm we were *part* of the pool. Felt like that to us too. It was a heavy worm, and quite a long one, but eventually the last of it slid off us and we hauled ourselves to our feet gasping for breath and trying to unclog our nostrils with our fingers. The slime was as sticky as glue, which meant that every part of us stuck to every other part. We were even stuck to each other. When one of us moved an arm, so did someone else. Strands of green gloop hung from our every bit. Even stretched between our lips when we tried to chat about it.

'Thiddithanurthingatheverappendamee!'[1] said Pete.

'ArterissInerrercmplainbouschkoolagen!'[2] (Me)

'Iwannagu-gu-gu-gu-gow*owm*!!!'[3] (Angie)

And then something new happened. Well, it had to, hadn't it? Things had been kind of quiet around there lately. The something new was that all the

---

[1] 'This is the worst thing that's ever happened to me!'

[2] 'After this I'll never complain about school again!'

[3] 'I want to go *home*!!!'

little flaps that had been letting light and air in suddenly slammed shut. Everything went dark. I mean *totally* dark. We couldn't even see one another's outlines.

I gulped down the last of the slime in my mouth and called to Pete and Angie. They didn't reply. I called again. They didn't reply again. I reached out, left and right. No one there. I felt behind me and in front of me. No one there either. I was alone. And...and there was something different. I felt my face, my clothes. Dry. Not sticky. It was as if the giant slug had never existed. So where was I? What was going on? And why was it so *dark*?

I was scared. Very scared.

Just as I was thinking of sinking to the ground and covering my head till everything returned to normal, a moon appeared. I mean literally appeared, like it had been switched on. It was only a bit of moon, a melon slice of a moon, floating in a window, but you have no *idea* how glad I was to see it. I would have gone to the window, looked out to try and guess where I was, but then more light appeared, from somewhere else. A tall upright crack of it that got slowly wider and wider until it stopped. Now I could see. The new light was from a fridge that had just opened all by itself. Our fridge. The McCue family fridge. I was in our kitchen. At home.

I gasped. I was at home? At night? But how?

There was only one explanation.

I'd been sleep-walking. I'd been tucked up in my bed and had got up, still asleep, come downstairs in the dark, splurged awake in the pitch-black kitchen. Which meant that I'd dreamt the slug.

I was so relieved about this that I did what any self-respecting kid would do if he happens to be in the kitchen at night without any Golden Oldies there telling him what he can and can't do. That fridge was practically begging to be raided, and I was the one to do it. I pulled the door further back. Looked inside.

There was no food in there. Nothing to drink even. But there was something. Two somethings. The kind of somethings that you don't normally find in fridges. One of these was a stick with a bit of card on the top. There were words on the card.

THIS SHOULD BE YOURS

But it wasn't the words that made my blood run cold. It was what the stick was standing up in.

A brain.

A human brain.

I closed my eyes tight.

And screamed.

chapter Twenty-nine

I was still screaming when I realised that I could see light through my eyelids. Not fridgelight. Not moon light. Daylight. I shut my mouth and opened my peepers. I was on the school playing field, and Pete and Angie were gawping at me. So were Atkins and his baldy buds from a little way off.

'What's with the hysterics?' Angie asked.

'Hyst...hyst...hysterics?'

'When the slug suddenly vanished you went all peculiar. Couldn't hear us, didn't seem able to see. Then you acted like you were pulling a door open even though there was no door. Then you screamed. Explain.'

I looked towards the houses along the edge of the field. At one house in particular. One window. Which still contained a certain spiky little head. He was watching me. To see what I'd do next.

I took out the piece of paper he'd given me. And

it came to me in a flash. What he wanted me to do.

'This message,' I said. 'It isn't the name of a Golden Oldie pop group. It's short for "you too".' I spelt it out in case they didn't get it.

'You too?' said Pete.

'Meaning me. Russell wants me to go through the same thing he thinks I put his brother through. The thing he thinks I danced for joy about. It's an eye for an eye sort of thing. A head for a head.'

'You mean...?' Angie glanced at the goalpost.

I nodded.

'Well he'll just have to go and whistle then, won't he?' she said.

'No.'

'No? What do you mean, no?'

'This has got to end,' I said. 'And if that's the only way...'

I started towards the goalpost. Angie came after me.

'Jig, you can't.'

I marched on. But stopped before I reached the goal. I mustn't mess this up. If I messed up, he might make it go on and on. It had to happen the way it happened before. Might not count if I just slapped my head on the goalpost. I needed a helper. I looked for Pete. He was already backing away. He'd seen the way my mind was going to work before I'd seen it myself. Who else then? Angie? No, it had to be a boy.

'Atkins!'

Eejit stopped trying to break the neck of the mate he'd just armlocked in the name of sport.

'Wot!'

'Need you to do something for me!'

He dropped his mate in surprise. I hardly ever ask Atkins to do anything for me, though he's forever offering. When we lived on Borderline Way we never had much to do with one another, but since we became neighbours on the Estate he asks at least once a week if he can join the Three Musketeers. I've tried explaining that 'Three' isn't clever code for 'Four', but the twonk still seems to live in hope.

'You wants me to do summink fer you?' he said.

'Yeh! Get over here! And bring one of your balls!'

He grabbed a football and scampered across with it.

'Whassup, Jig?'

'I want you to stand against that goalpost while I head butt you,' I said.

'Ya do?'

'Yes.'

'Why?'

'I just do.'

'One fer all and all fer lunch, eh?'

'That's it, Eej.'

He trotted to the goalpost.

'Got your phone with you?' I asked Angie.

'Yes, but—'

'The hospital is still open for emergencies on Sundays, isn't it?'

'Yes, till next year, when it's turned into a prison. But Jig, you can't do this.'

'Got to,' I said.

I went to the goal and took the ball off Atkins. Stood him against the post exactly the way I'd stood last Wednesday afternoon. I even folded his arms across his chest for him.

'What is it?' he asked. 'Some sorta game, like?'

'Yeah, that's right.'

'Wot I gotta do then?'

'All you have to do is stand there while I run at you like I'm going to lob my fine head of hair at your baldness, and just before we make contact you step aside – clear?'

'Clear,' he said, all teeth. 'Then kin I be a Muskiteer?'

'You have to apply in writing,' I said.

'Writing?'

'Block capitals'll do.'

I turned to face the Ryans' house. Russell was still watching. I held the ball over my head to make sure he'd get the idea. Then I dropped it on my toe, like Mr Rice keeps trying to show us. The idea is that when you've dropped the ball on your toe, your toe kicks it north, then your head knocks it back onto your toe, then your toe kicks it northward again, then your head knocks it back onto your toe, and so on and so on while you wonder what the hell this has to do with education. I dropped the ball onto my toe. It glanced off the side of my shoe and dropped to the ground in a sulk. I let it lie. Just hoped Russell understood. If he didn't, I could be in for a big headache for nothing.

I told Atkins not to move a muscle or pore until I was as close as could be to butting his head with mine.

'OK, Jig,' he said cheerfully.

I took a bunch of steps back, then ran on the spot for a bit the way Bry-Ry does. I glanced one last time at Russell in the window, then headed for the goalpost. I didn't want to think about what I was going to do. Didn't dare or I'd chicken out. As I ran, I put everything out of my mind except that I was going to head-butt Eejit Atkins, the way Ryan must have imagined he was going to head-butt me. It was important to get that right or Russell might pick up on it and give me the thumbs down.

I was almost there. Atkins stood just like I'd told him, arms folded. He still had that big stupid grin on his face.

I put on a spurt.

A metre and a half short of the goal I launched myself off the ground.

I flew through the air.

Any second now Eejit would step aside, my head would smash against the goalpost, I'd fall to the ground and—

That was the last thing I knew until I woke up.

Chapter Thirty

It was evening. The lights were on. But they weren't my bedroom lights. Wasn't my bed either. My bed's softer. So…?

Without moving my head — I didn't dare yet — I looked around. Another bed over to the left. Empty. I rolled my eyes the other way. Bed there too, someone in that one, facing away from me. My nose felt weird. There was something up it. I downed my eyes to my chest. Wires suckered to it. I looked at my hands. A peg on one of my finger ends. I turned my head, very carefully. A screen with three lines rising and falling, quietly going pip-pip-pip…

My scheme had worked! I was in hospital!

It wasn't the same room Ryan had been in, but like him I'd banged my head on the goalpost when the person standing there stepped aside, lost consciousness, been bundled off to hospital when Angie called an ambulance. If Russell wouldn't leave me alone after this, he never would.

But then a worry popped into my head. What if this was one of Russell's set-ups? What if I wasn't in hospital but on my back on the playing field while he stuffed all this into my mind. If I was in an imaginary bed in an imaginary hospital, any minute now an imaginary bulldozer could come through the wall and make me part of the imaginary mattress. How could I find out if I was safe from Russell's revenge? I looked around for some clue. There had to be something...

On my little bedside table there were half a dozen cards. Get Well cards obviously. Maybe there'd be something in one of them, like a message from someone Russell couldn't know about. I was just reaching for a couple of the cards when I heard a familiar voice.

'Jig!'

It came from the other occupied bed. Someone I knew only too well was sitting up in it.

'Eejit?'

'Finally come to then, 'as ya?' Atkins said. 'I come aat of it yesterdy.'

'Eejit, what are you doing here?'

313

'You should know, mate, you wuz the one wot put me 'ere.'

'Me?'

'When you banged me 'ead.'

'Banged your head?'

'When you stood me by the goal and charged me.'

'Atkins, you were supposed to move! You were supposed to step aside!'

He grinned moronically. 'I fort you wuz jokin' abaat that.'

'You thought I was joking about you getting out of the way when my head was coming at you at fifty-six miles an hour? Why would you think that? Why would you stay there and *be* butted, you cretin?'

'Well, it wuz a game, wunnit? Said so yerself.'

I groaned. So it hadn't happened the way I planned it. I hadn't headed the goalpost, I'd headed Eejit Atkins. Had my efforts been in vain after all?

'Hey! McCue! Ya made it!'

Another familiar voice. I lifted my head carefully from the pillow. Didn't want to lose the thing in my

314

nose or the wires on my chest. Didn't want those pips to stop. I looked at the person who'd come in to the bay. It was Ryan. In a dressing gown.

'I heard you were here,' he said, coming closer. 'You and me both, whaddayaknow.'

'And me!' Atkins squawked from the other bed.

'Yeah, and you,' Ryan said.

'You're awake,' I said to him.

'Glad it shows,' he said.

'What's the last thing you remember before you woke up?'

'Um…nattering to you in soccer practice.'

'Can't remember cracking your head on the goalpost?'

'No. Wish I could.'

'You wish you could remember cracking your head? Ryan, are you as insane as Atkins?'

'Jiggy!'

Familiar voice number three. My mother, with my dad riding her heels. She looked like she was going to detonate with happiness as she approached my bed. She bent over me and kissed my cheek. Then she pulled a chair up, sat down, took my hand. The one without the finger peg.

'Sight for sore eyes, you are,' Dad said, keeping his distance. 'Conscious, I mean.' None of that sloppy stuff for my old man, I'm glad to say.

Mum looked at Ryan. 'How are you today, Bryan?'

'I'm good,' he answered. 'One more day and I'm outta here.'

'That's terrific.' She turned to Eejit, sitting up in the other bed. 'And you, Ralph? How are you doing?'

'Great,' Atkins said. 'S'better 'ere than at 'ome. Ya git waited on 'ere.'

'How long have I been here?' I asked my parents.

Mum squeezed my hand. 'Since Sunday.'

'Which was…?'

'Three days ago.'

'Three days!'

'Three and a half to be precise. You boys and your games. What were you even *doing* on school premises on a Sunday, that's what I want to know.'

'Leave it out, Peg,' said Dad. 'Wait till he's home for the grand inquisition. Give him something to look forward to.'

'Oh, Jiggy,' Mum said. 'I was so worried.'

There were tears in her eyes as she gripped my hand even tighter. If she squeezed much harder there'd be one or two in mine too.

'Three days,' I murmured. 'So it's Wednesday.'

'Yes.'

'Another Wednesday.'

'That's right.'

'But that means...'

I glanced at the cards on the bedside table. They weren't Get Well cards, they were birthday cards. Yesterday's birthday cards.

'There are lots of presents waiting for you at home,' Mum said. 'We would have brought some tonight if we'd known you were awake. Happy birthday, darling.'

'Yeah, happy birthday, kid,' Dad said. 'How's it feel to be in double figures?'

'Double figures?'

'Thirteen. A teenager.'

I looked at my father with pity. 'Dad, I've been in double figures since I turned ten.'

He worked it out. 'So you have.'

'My mum was in earlier with a birthday card for you,' Ryan said.

He felt in a pocket of his dressing gown and handed me a blue envelope. I opened it. Took out the card. On the front was a picture of a footballer. Ryan grinned.

'Guess my little brother chose it.'

I looked inside. Mrs Ryan had written 'From all of us, get well soon, dear.' Underneath this, another hand had written...

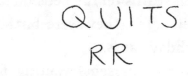

QUITS
RR

I sighed with relief. It really was over.

I put the card with the others.

'Angie and Pete have visited you every day after school,' Mum said. 'They'll be thrilled to know you've come round.'

'They'd better be,' I said. 'Did they talk to me?'

'Talk to you?'

'While I was dead to the world.'

'Why would they do that?'

'To help me back to consciousness. Either that or to get a few things off their manky chests.'

'You'll have to ask them.'

'Oh, I will.'

'Now I think we should hold hands and sing Happy Birthday,' Mum said.

'What?'

She said it again.

'Do that,' I said, 'and I leave home as soon as they let me out of here.'

She laughed and gave her spare hand to Dad.

'Kin I join in?' Eejit asked excitedly.

'No one's joining in,' I said. 'Mum. Dad. You do not want to do this.'

'Oh, but we do,' Mum said. 'It's a big thing, becoming a teenager. You don't want to forget *this* birthday, do you?'

'I already have. Slept through it, remember?'

Dad was about to take my other hand when Mum nudged him with her eyes, then flipped the same eyes to Ryan. She wanted him included. Dad wasn't too comfortable with this, you could tell, but it was a special occasion, so he offered Ryan his hand.

'Bryan?' Mum said gently.

Ryan smirked at me. I knew what that smirk meant. We were in hospital recovering from almost identical injuries collected on the school playing field. For the first time in our lives we had something in common other than being useless at maths. He took Dad's hand – and mine.*

Then Mum started to sing. Well, sing. Make that horrible racket she *calls* singing. My pip-pip-pip screen went berserk. Dad joined in to drown her out. So did Ryan. 'Happy Birthday, dear Jiggy,' they sang.

Yes, Bryan Ryan, archest of all my enemies, was holding my hand and calling me dear! The world had gone mad.

When Atkins added his screechy little voice to the rest a couple of nurses ran in to see if one of their patients was being strangled by lunatics. When they saw that I was awake they skidded to a halt, beamed, and *also* joined in.

I think I blushed.

Still. The bright side.

It's the day after my thirteenth birthday and I'm legitimately off school during term-time. In bed too, and not feeling bad in spite of the tubes and wires and all the rest. If I play it right I can really milk this hospital gig. Be off school and excused the parental nagging and homework

---
* This time the only shock was that we were holding hands.

for a week, maybe even longer.

In bed, people visiting me, being nice to me, singing to me.

And tomorrow they'll bring me presents.

Unlucky thirteen? Don't you believe it!

Jiggy McCue

(Teenager)

Turn the page
to find out about
Jiggy McCue's other
wildly wacky
adventures...

The Poltergoose

A Jiggy McCue Story

Michael Lawrence

£4.99

1 86039 836 7

Something's after Jiggy McCue!
Something big and angry and invisible.
Something which hisses and flaps and stabs
his bum and generally tries to make
his life a misery. Where did it come from?

Jiggy calls together the Three Musketeers
– One for all and all for lunch! –
and they set out to send the poltergoose
back where it belongs.

Shortlisted for the Blue Peter Book Award

The underpants from hell – that's what
Jiggy calls them, and not just because they
look so gross. No, these pants are evil.
And they're in control. Of him. Of his life!
Can Jiggy get to the bottom of his
problem before it's too late?

"...the funniest book I've ever read."
Teen Titles
"Hilarious!"
The *Independent*
Winner of the Stockton Children's
Book of the Year Award

A Jiggy McCue Story

The Toilet of Doom

Michael Lawrence

1 84121 752 2   £4.99

Feel like your life has gone down the pan?
Well here's your chance to swap it
for a better one!

When those tempting words appear on the
computer screen, Jiggy McCue just can't
resist. He hits "F for Flush" and... Oh dear.
He really shouldn't have done that. Because
the life he gets in place of his own is a very
embarrassing one – for a boy.

"Fast, furious and full of good humour."
National Literacy Association
"Altogether good fun." *School Librarian*
"Hilarity and confusion."

A Jiggy McCue Story

Maggot Pie

1 84121 756 5   £4.99

Michael Lawrence

Jiggy McCue wants some good
luck for a change.
But instead of luck he gets a genie.
A teenage genie who turns against him.
Then the maggoty dreams start.
Dreams which, with his luck and this genie,
might just come true.

"Will have you squirming with horror and delight!"
Ottakars 8-12 Book of the Month
"Funny, wacky and lively."
cool-reads.co.uk

When the new girl in Jiggy's class sneezes
her nose explodes. Runny nose stuff
everywhere. If you look in the runny nose
stuff you can see the future.

Pity the future is always bad.

But the little round creature from the dump
doesn't care. Future Snot is his favourite
meal. He just laps it up!

1 84362 647 0   £4.99

Jiggy McCue's clothes keep
disappearing – in public. Suddenly,
when there are teachers, friends,
neighbours and total strangers
about, he hasn't a stitch on.

What's causing this? And what can
Jiggy, Pete and Angie do to stop it?

All is revealed in Jiggy's most
embarrassing adventure yet!

**Winner of the Doncaster Children's Book Award
and the Solihull Children's Book Award**

When Jiggy, Pete and Angie go on the wrong holiday, Jiggy has a feeling that something bad is about to happen.

How right he is!

An old enemy is pulling their strings, making them dance to his tune.

Turn the page to see
some other funny books
from Orchard that
you might enjoy...

"Let's write a joke book!"

It was just one of those ideas that took off. Julian and
his friends thought writing a joke book would be easy.
But hundreds of corny **groan-out-loud**
jokes later, they're not so sure...

This hilarious and touching story, full of everyone's
favourite old jokes – and some new ones! – is
guaranteed to have you **howling with laughter**.

"Sensitive and lighthearted. Kids will love it. And if you
must know, it's an underwear-wolf!" **Books for Keeps**

"This book gloriously manages to be both sad and funny."
Booktrust 100 Best Books

EMILY SMITH

1 84121 810 3

£4.99

Jeff really liked television. Cartoons were more interesting than life. Sit coms were funnier than life. And in life you never got to watch someone trying to ride a bike over an open sewer. Sometimes at night Jeff even dreamed television. Mum complained, but it didn't make any difference. Jeff didn't take any notice of her, which was a mistake.

A very funny and thought-provoking book from Emily Smith, winner of two Smarties Prizes.

Shortlisted for the Blue Peter Book Award.

orchard Red Apples

Orchard Red Apples are available from all good bookshops,
or can be ordered direct from the publisher:
Orchard Books, PO Box 29, Douglas, IM99 1BQ
Credit card orders please telephone 01624 836000
or fax 01624 837033 or visit our Internet site: www.wattspub.co.uk
or email: bookshop@enterprise.net for details.

To order please quote title, author and ISBN
and your full name and address.
Cheques and postal orders should be made payable to
'Bookpost plc'.
Postage and packing is FREE within the UK
(overseas customers should add £1.00 per book).
Prices and availability are subject to change.